This was her river, smack-dab in the middle of Mississippi. Unpredictable and unsafe, it stank when rain stirred its thick sludge of mud beneath brown pebbles and river stones. Its currents were hidden, dangerous to those foolish enough to jump into those waters without so much as a limb tossed in to discover what couldn't be seen.

She'd done her best to understand. To find that limb and toss it into unknown waters. Once again, it had been too late. And not enough.

Praise for *RIVER'S CALL*

"Missy is young. Gangly. Awkward. But when the river deposits a small town's secrets onto her muddy shore, Missy becomes something else. Dangerous. This story will sweep you into dark secrets flowing under the currents of a river and behind the smiles of people Missy has known all her life. Taut with intrigue, you too will be transformed by *RIVER'S CALL*."

~Melanie Hemry, author

~*~

"With the Southern flavor of *To Kill A Mockingbird*, this historical mystery is intriguing and achingly authentic."

~Robin Patchen, author

River's Call

by

Laurel Thomas

River's Call

Contact Information: info@thewildrosepress.com

Cover Art by *Abigail Owen*

The Wild Rose Press, Inc.
PO Box 708
Adams Basin, NY 14410-0708
Visit us at www.thewildrosepress.com

Publishing History
First Vintage Rose Edition, 2019
Print ISBN 978-1-5092-2758-7
Digital ISBN 978-1-5092-2759-4

Published in the United States of America

Dedication

To my husband,
who loved the story of *River's Call*
before it was all spiffed up.
And who has loved me the same way.

Chapter 1

"There's quicksand in Mississippi. If you step in it, Pa says the last thing you should do is fight. Struggle and you're sunk. So if you get caught, best thing you can do is nothin'."

Raindrops pelted Missy's forehead and woke her. Another storm. She bent forward to close the window and saw oak branches jump in wild tangos through flashes of lightning. Sounds in the distance rose above the storm.

Voices? Maybe some drunk was pitchin' a fit on Main Street. Or, more likely, a bobcat screamed over its prey. Sometimes, a storm carried voices on its wings downriver.

"Pa's knife!"

She'd borrowed it yesterday. Except *borrow* wasn't exactly the word Pa would use. It was his grandfather's knife, engraved with the same initials that belonged to Pa. He kept it tucked away in his socks drawer. Missy wouldn't have touched it, much less used it. But she'd lost her best whittlin' knife, and her piece for the county fair had to be done by Friday. She'd told herself she'd remember to bring it back. Pa'd never know it was gone.

But when the river had beckoned her for a late afternoon wade along its pebbled beach, she'd tucked the knife at the base of a river oak and forgotten it. Her stomach lurched. Pa'd open that socks drawer in the morning. What if he figured out his knife was gone?

The last thing she wanted was to go out in the dark. And in the rain. Typhoid fever raged in a rainy environment. And mosquitoes and malaria. And wanton criminal types.

Then again, she'd forgotten something else long ago. What she'd lost hurt so bad, she'd promised herself never to forget again. Not that it had helped. Still, she was going to get that knife back. Tonight.

At least she could bring Ranger. At sixty pounds of young pit bull mutt, her dog looked scarier than he was. Nobody had to know he was a cupcake inside.

She'd run to the river with Ranger, get the knife, and be back before Pa was up. Changing into shorts and T-shirt, she then grabbed a flashlight from under her bed. A rain slicker peeked out from under the nearest pile of clothes. After throwing it on, she hung the flashlight from a cord around her neck.

She turned to her doorway and stopped. A quiet walk downstairs was impossible. The old stairs creaked and groaned with every step. No way could she tiptoe out without waking Pa. She looked out the window and sighed, then climbed onto a thick branch outside her window and slid from one lower branch to another before she landed on slushy ground.

In the yellow glow of the outdoor security light, Ranger pulled on a frayed rope that tethered him near the shed. He greeted her with happy wiggles, his brindle coat drenched and matted.

"Come on, boy. You can help."

She struggled to untie the wet rope from Ranger's

collar that held him to the metal stay. Her hands slipped as Ranger stretched his head to lick her.

"Stop slobbering!" With one more yank, the knot untangled. Ranger lunged through the battered door of the shed without a look behind. He headed for the farthest corner and curled himself into the smallest version of himself he could manage. Like she couldn't see him anymore.

"Nice try, you ninny. Come with me." Missy pointed her finger at him. "Now."

He didn't move.

She stomped her foot. "Dang it. I said *now*."

Ranger burrowed his behind into the corner. When she tried to yank him forward by his front haunches, he planted front paws and didn't budge.

"Coward. What about all those times I brought you water on hot days? Played catch just to make you happy? And *now* when I need you?"

Ranger whimpered and looked at her with pleading brown eyes, still immovable.

Missy shifted her tactics. Anger wasn't working on his pea-brain. Neither was guilt.

"Come on. I'll give you a treat." She pulled her hand out of a pocket, pretending there was some unknown juicy morsel.

Ranger perked up his ears at the word *treat*. He shifted toward her. Missy grabbed him around the belly and pulled. He sat and, as they both plopped onto the wooden floor, he licked her ear.

He wasn't going anywhere.

Missy shone the flashlight into the darkness outside. Rain poured in rivulets over the shed door. Maybe she'd just forget it. Then she imagined Pa rummaging through his socks in the morning. Pulling her rain slicker closer, she drew in a breath and ran into the night.

Dodging in and out of trees, she ran until she heard the river, the rush of floodwaters spilling over its banks. Quicksand was sure to form somewhere. She remembered that Pa'd said to look out for places where the banks had overflowed and then receded. She should be okay.

An abandoned warehouse loomed nearby. One she usually steered clear of after the first time she'd peeked inside. Mice had skittered between broken bottles, and slats of aged tin clapped against each other.

Rumors were it was haunted. Kids talked about some ghost who screamed in high-pitched wails on moonlit nights. Even gave her a name. Whatever. Still, when she'd heard a vehicle pull up to its ancient doors that day, she'd run.

Lights flashed now in weird contortions through gaps in the old timbers. Who'd be at the warehouse this time of night? She dimmed her flashlight and hid behind several old trash cans around the back of the building.

Shrouded figures came into focus. They gathered around something lying on the ground, kicking and shouting.

Was it a man? It looked like a doll, jerking with each kick, limbs bent at odd angles. Whatever it was, it was too broken to resist the blows coming from every direction.

Then she heard his cry.

She'd heard one like that before. When Pa'd put down her horse, Old Blackie. She'd tried to shut out the animal's scream, but it had snatched her heart and pried open her eyes. All she could do was watch, helpless to save the horse she loved.

But this was a man crying. For mercy. For help. Still, the blows kept coming. His cries became moans in time that had suspended. Missy felt a soft bed of mud creep around her like a shroud. Wrapping arms around her body tight, she tried to stop it from rocking in giant quakes.

She closed her eyes so she could leave, if only in her mind. Instead, she was caught in a horror movie she couldn't escape. As the beating continued, the moans grew softer. When an arm jabbed up and down, blade glinting in the moonlight, the body became still.

Muttered oaths replaced angry shouts. The storm quieted as if it were weary. Rain slowed to a drizzle. Finally, silence crept in like a sigh of relief.

Missy couldn't move, couldn't breathe. Lights bobbed away into the night. Except for one solitary beam. A man stood over the body. He lifted a wide-brimmed hat as he peered down and nodded, content with the evening's business. Then, he turned and left.

Missy's body ached as she sat, rolled into a ball. She heard car doors creak, then close. Engines started and gears shifted as the attackers drove off. She chanced a breath, then another, and waited till all she heard was the departing storm.

What if he ain't dead?

Everything inside her wanted to run. To pretend like she hadn't seen a man beaten to a pulp. What could she do? Maybe she'd run home and get Pa. He'd know what to do.

But how could she leave someone alone and

broken in the night?

No more lights danced in angry waves. Rotating in the wet ground, she listened for movement in the river grass, behind trees and in the dense vegetation. No traffic drove by on the county road over the ridge. Only the call of a nightingale sounded.

After a deep breath, Missy ducked around the trash cans and headed to a broken door that swung on its hinges. She turned her flashlight on and crept closer. It looked like they'd dumped their victim to one side. She stood and walked into the warehouse, pointing the flashlight's beam toward the battered form.

Gravel crunched from the back of the warehouse, and her heart stopped. The movement came from behind a rusty beam. In the shaft of her flashlight, a man walked toward her. She recognized his hat. It was the man she'd last seen peering down at the body.

"Come here, girl," he said.

Missy stood frozen, as if a hypnotist beckoned. His voice was muted, like he'd covered his mouth. But she could almost make out his features. Just a few more steps, and she'd memorize the set of those eyes and attach them to a person.

"Come. Here. Now." His command drew her like an invisible wire of a marionette master. He pulled and she obeyed. Until a tiny glimpse of light flickered in Missy's heart.

It was something Mama'd told her. She'd been so little she couldn't remember it at first. She'd been afraid of the dark. Of storms. Of any shadow that lurked in her closet. The memory of Mama's words whispered now.

Courage will come, little one. If you let it.

She flipped off the flashlight and ran. Crashing

through the door into darkness, she tripped on debris outside the warehouse, let out a cry, then sprinted away. She ducked in and out of the cover of trees and undergrowth.

Diving into the middle of a dense line of cattails, she curled into a knot and made herself small. Behind her, the man cursed and slashed through leaves and branches.

Looking up above the long stems, she saw the sky had become a dark slate. Dawn would bring morning light. It was only a matter of time before he'd find her.

"You can't hide from me," he said. The wind in the trees took his words and carried them to her. She couldn't tell which direction they came from, only that they were like a hiss that hovered in the darkness. They drove a spear into her gut.

"Better not tell, girl. I'll make you pay," he said. "With the one you love most."

Her tears were so hot, she wondered if steam rose off her cold skin. The woods that had been her refuge since she was little were fixin' to become her coffin. If only she'd memorized every tree, every shift in the land, she'd be able to find her way out. But it was still too dark.

The man's movement through the brush faded. Missy heard the sound of gravel shifting at the riverbank.

She stood and, with one long leap, sprinted away. A break in the woods beckoned in the gray light. Hurtling long legs, one after the other, she ran until the green asbestos roof of home appeared through misty treetops.

Home had never felt so far away. Gasping for

breath, she broke out of the woods and into the open field that signaled their land. She kept running until the front gate of home appeared. Charging through the gate, she tripped on a hoe hidden in the yard and collapsed in the damp grass.

The front door slammed, and she heard her dad.

"I've been worried sick."

It was his angry, scared voice. Like when she'd run in front of that car, old enough to know better. Pa knelt beside her. He pulled tangled red hair out of her face and glared.

"Just about called Sheriff Davis. Where've you been?"

"The warehouse at the river…Go look."

She twisted, head over sweet pea vines, and threw up. Her curls were splattered as she heaved in the grass. Pa clambered up the porch steps, and the door slammed behind him. She heard the rotary dial of the phone and Pa's voice through the screen door.

"Emmett. Hal Needham here. Missy's seen something at the old Beemon warehouse by the river. Best get over here."

Minutes later, a squad car spun gravel as it pulled into the drive.

"Hop in," the sheriff yelled.

Pa jogged to the car and climbed in. Gravel sprayed into the morning air as the car drove away.

After crawling to the spigot, Missy turned on the tap and let cool water run over her head and face, washing away the mud and sick and leaving her shivering. She didn't know how long she'd sat there by the time Pa slammed the door of the squad car and headed toward her. Emmett climbed out of the car and stood, waiting.

Pa crouched beside her. He started in a low tone with careful words, placed like thread through his best fishing pole. "It was Ephraim Moriah. He's dead."

Ephraim. Her friend. She remembered his kind smile, the whittlin' contests they'd had.

The man she'd seen at the warehouse, the one who'd chased her, had murdered her friend.

Missy wrapped her arms around her legs and hid her face. The smell of warm earth, tears, and sweat mixed up with the lie she'd decided to tell. She'd heard the man's threats.

And Pa was the one she loved most.

Chapter 2

How had the man known what would freeze her into silence? Had he recognized her in the darkness?

She'd never tell what she'd seen that night. She'd pretend. She'd pretend so good, no one would ever know.

"What happened?" Pa sat with his long arm circling her shoulders. "Why were you at the river so early?"

"I was up... wanted to take a walk by the river before school. I...I didn't know who he was." Missy kept her eyes from his, in case he saw the lie and pulled it out.

"Did you notice anyone else?"

Missy turned her head away and dry-heaved into the grass.

"Come inside." He turned to the sheriff standing nearby. "Emmett, we'll talk later."

"But I need..."

"She's fourteen. Give me some time here."

Pa helped her to her feet and tucked her under his arm. They watched as mud flew from the back tires of the squad car. It fishtailed, then caught gravel and drove away. Missy's tears mixed with a circle of sweat under Pa's arm as he led her into the house and toward her bedroom.

She hesitated by the bathroom door. Mama

would've piled her into a tub of warm, soapy water. But that was a long time ago. She slipped into bed where damp curls met warm pillow and sleep overtook the pain.

Her eyes didn't open until sun had faded in burnished light through her window. She heard Pa's boots trudging up the stairs. He knocked on the door once, then opened it, balancing a tray with toast, a mug of milk, and some sort of pill.

"Doc Matthews sent this over."

Missy swallowed the pill with sips of the warm milk. She tasted the tangy sweetness of the sorghum he'd added. It traveled into her belly and settled its warmth there.

"Emmett's gonna have to talk to you sometime soon. Investigation can't wait much longer."

Missy looked up, panicked.

"Has to be done," he said. "Go back to sleep now, hear?"

She didn't wake up until she smelled bacon frying downstairs the next morning. By the time she'd showered and hobbled to the kitchen, Pa was slapping his arms with a dish towel as bacon grease splattered. He plopped down a plate of scorched pancakes and crispy bacon on the kitchen table. Missy looked up in unbelief.

"Beggars can't be choosers. Eat."

Her body ached, but her belly was empty and complaining. Tears spilled and overflowed as the syrup dripped over burnt edges. When Pa touched her shoulder, it unlocked a gusher inside. She bent over and sobbed.

"Anything you can remember from that morning?

Anything at all?"

The screen door in the kitchen rattled, and a voice called, "Sheriff here."

"Emmett." Pa opened the door. They faced each other toe to toe against an invisible line.

"She ready?" Sheriff Davis glanced at her, pen and notebook in hand.

"For a few questions," her dad answered.

Missy wiped her face with her hands and straightened her shoulders. She looked at the two men. Pa was as tall and lanky as Emmett was stout and squat. An old tension crept around the edges every time they met, whether it was a nod from the steering wheel as they passed on a county road or a chance meeting at the town square.

Felt like they'd be on the floor wrestling right now, if they had the chance. Pa said they'd competed against each other in football. Missy wondered what else they'd fought over. Neither one seemed like the backin' down kind. Even now, Pa watched Emmett like a mama bear as the sheriff sat across from Missy with a notebook in his stumpy fingers.

"How you feelin'?"

Missy knew it was only a polite way to start the questioning. She prayed a quick prayer for help in the cover-up.

"Okay," Missy said.

Emmett looked at her and waited. Missy kept her eyes fixed on a crack in the wall just beyond the sheriff's head.

"Hope you didn't see that mess. Heard you were at the river." Sheriff Davis didn't take his eyes off Missy. He was studying her.

After taking in a giant gulp of air, she blew it out and grabbed another.

War was going on inside. She wanted to tell everything she knew. But how could she? What if the law wasn't big enough to protect Pa? It hadn't been big enough to protect Ephraim.

"Yes, sir." Missy forced the two words out. Looking for a distraction, she settled on a clump of eyebrow that drooped into the sheriff's eyes.

"Tell me what you saw." The sheriff tapped his pen against his leg.

Missy tried not to suck in another long breath. Maybe she could press the memory out by thinking about something else. But the harder she thought, the clearer became the image of the mob and Ephraim, alone and helpless.

"It was dark, raining," she said.

"Raining? Rain let up around five in the morning." Sheriff Davis fired his questions like a pistol. Missy needed time to think, but he knew that. He interrogated criminals all the time. He knew she was dodging his questions.

"I was scared." Her gaze shifted back to the crack in the wall.

"Anybody else around?" The sheriff kept his eyes directed on hers.

"I didn't know who…it was." A fine line of sweat appeared over her upper lip.

"Didn't know who it was? You didn't recognize the body? Or you saw someone else?"

"I…it was dark."

"That don't make sense." The sheriff made a note on his paper. "The rain was over around five. Sun came up around six. Should've been able to see. What are you hiding, girl?"

Missy pulled her arms around her chest. She quaked as if Emmett were trying to shake the answers out of her.

"Stop." Pa held his hand up and stepped closer to Missy.

Emmett Davis hit the table with his fist. "This is a murder investigation. If she saw something or someone, I need to know."

Missy felt her dad's eyes rest on her. He paused, then spoke. "We're done here."

After an awkward silence, Emmett pushed back in his chair and stood. "I'll be back." The screen door slammed behind him, and boots slapped the wooden porch.

Pa sat beside her. He waited until the engine noise from the sheriff's car faded, then whirled to face Missy. "What's going on?"

"I don't know." Missy's words were stuck inside. Her head felt like the nest of baby mice she'd found under the kitchen sink one day. Bits and pieces of who knew what, all meshed together.

"I can't sort it out, Pa. I can't."

Pa waited another minute, then stood and walked to the phone. A moment later, he spoke into the receiver.

"Mr. Jeremiah Lucas, please. Hal Needham here. Need to speak with him as soon as possible."

After a short pause he said, "Need an appointment."

The Jeremiah Lucas. His name was on every benefit, on every city council vote, and on billboards all over town during elections. Not that he had much competition. He was handsome, rich, and white. A winning combination.

Except for one thing, Jeremiah Lucas had it all.

Missy remembered Lucy, his little girl. Her round face had grinned up at everyone on downtown's cobblestoned streets. Over the years her body grew, but her mind stayed behind at the playground, never moving into the adult world.

Missy guessed she was more fun than life deserved because she up and disappeared one day after school. Never did find out what happened. Pretty Jessica Daly, Jeremiah's wife, left a few weeks after that. All that charity work, and now Mr. Lucas was alone with a sullen hulk of a son in a small town filled with old biddies and local nobodies who talked about every hidden morsel and tidbit of information. The ones they knew and the ones they made up.

Mr. Lucas had contacts all over the country. According to Pa, he'd used them to look for his daughter. But she'd never been found.

No telling what Pa wanted to talk to him about. Or which answers she'd need ready on her tongue. Except Mr. Lucas had lost a little girl. Maybe he'd understand about a scared one. Like her.

Emmett hadn't been anything but the law, trying to get answers. Sure, she was keeping quiet when he needed to figure out what'd happened. Emmett didn't know about losing someone, though. But Mr. Lucas did.

All her strength had drained out. Yet she couldn't sleep, didn't dare close her eyes for fear of what she'd see replayed in her mind over and over. She leaned against a pillow resting on the wall beside her bed and pulled an old half-used spiral notebook from under her bed. Maybe if she could write a script, then memorize it, no one would figure out she was lying.

She wrote scene after scene, tearing each one up and tossing it on the floor as soon as it was written. These weren't the doodles and sunshiny day meanderings of stories she jotted down just for fun. They were desperate pleas for a hidden place when questions fired like buck shot and she didn't know where to duck. When she finally slept, the alarm blared.

Ready or not.

After breakfast, Missy rubbed her eyes and stared out the passenger window of Pa's pickup as they headed to the attorney's office. Loblolly pines stood alongside the road like giant sentinels guarding swampy marshland. She checked her watch as Pa pulled into a driveway.

White foam and turquoise of a fountain signaled the circle drive of a restored plantation home. After they parked and climbed out, they passed planters of ivy on the wide veranda to the front door. Pa straightened his shoulders and retucked his shirt before he pressed the doorbell. An elderly woman with blue-gray hair and penciled lips greeted them.

"Good morning," she said, extending her hand. "Miss Jean Culpepper from the Hawk's Landing Culpeppers. I believe I knew your sweet wife, Mattie. We attended the Ladies Aid Society together. Every month for, well, you know, until…"

"Yes, ma'am." Pa lowered his gaze to the wooden porch slats. "She did love her lady's groups."

Miss Jean shook her head, and one piece of hair crept out of her tight up-swept roll and dangled on her neck. She sighed, "She was the picture of loveliness. She sure was."

Pa shifted on one foot and fidgeted with his collar. The tan line that made his neck always look red was hidden beneath a seldom-worn dress shirt. Probably hadn't been out of the closet since Mama's funeral.

"We have an appointment with Mr. Lucas at eight o'clock." Pa glanced at his watch, reminding Miss Culpepper of their purpose.

"Of course. Come on inside." Missy felt cool marble tile as they walked under a glittering crystal chandelier and through the foyer into an outer office.

A bottle of "I Dream Pink" nail polish sat on the desk next to an open copy of *Dark Romance*. Miss Jean spoke into an intercom, and Mr. Lucas stepped out of his private office. He beckoned them inside and closed the door.

"Mr. Needham. Missy. How are y'all?" He walked forward and shook their hands as if he'd been looking forward to their visit all morning.

"Just fine. 'Cept for all this rain," said Pa.

"Two inches in the rain gauge last night. More than we usually see this time of year. Have a seat."

Pa and Missy sat in leather upholstered chairs across from the scrolled mahogany desk. Mr. Lucas sat with a confident plop into his rolling office chair.

Missy'd never seen such a beautiful room. The walls were paneled with rich oak and lined with bookcases. Her feet sank into plush carpet. She shivered in the cool air from real air-conditioning. No window units here.

Floor-to-ceiling windows overlooked the manicured lawn and sparkling fountain in the back yard. Missy wondered if anyone got to hang out there. Like if Clarence and his dad played catch on its soft grass after school. That was hard to imagine. Still, that's what she and Pa did on days when the temperatures cooled from summer's blistering heat and before winter set in. Mr. Lucas followed her gaze and smiled. She was relieved when he turned his attention back to Pa.

"Guess we know why we're here," said Mr. Lucas. "A body found in the Beemon warehouse?"

"Yes, sir," answered Pa. "Ephraim Moriah."

"Tell me about that morning."

"I got up early. Nothing strange about that until I checked on Missy and she wasn't in her room. It was too early to be outside, even for her."

Missy stared at her knees, but she felt Pa's gaze. She couldn't bring herself to look up and meet it.

Pa continued. "I was heading out to look when I saw her sprawled out in the front yard."

Another long pause, as if they were waiting for her to say something. She kept staring at her knobby knees.

"She hasn't talked much. Won't hurt to have some representation. Don't know how she could be implicated in all this, but I want to make sure she's covered."

Representation? Could she get in trouble, be blamed? The world was spinning with her in it. Suddenly her head joined in, and the room around her swirled. Missy buried her face in her arms and leaned over, panicked as dizziness took control. She put her head between her knees as the school nurse had told her to do once. But her head kept spinning and her stomach kept churning. She tried to stand, make a run for the bathroom. But it was too late. She threw up on the brown and gold scrolls of an Oriental carpet.

"Dagnammit," she heard Pa mumble.

She wanted to hide but couldn't move. Closing her eyes, she willed the room to stop spinning. A tunnel got darker and darker until everything was black. She felt the descent onto soft, stinky fibers. Then pain as her head hit the desk.

According to Pa, it got pretty dramatic after that. Miss Jean had called the ambulance. They'd stuffed her in the back and taken off for the hospital. Too bad she'd missed it.

When she opened her eyes, she was attached to an IV with Pa's strong hand resting on her arm. "What happened?"

"Took a little tumble at Mr. Lucas's office."

She closed her eyes. "Pa, I…"

"Missy, how are you?" She looked up to see Mr. Lucas in the doorway. "Gave us a scare this morning."

She fought to stay awake, needed to watch out for Pa. To protect him. She couldn't afford to be out right now. Except her eyes wouldn't stay open and her head still spun as she tried to lift it from the pillow. A shadow chased her as she descended into blackness.

"No! He's all I got," she tried to shout. But the shadow and darkness mixed up in one big heap, and the last thing she heard was Pa's voice.

"What? I can't hear you," she heard him say. He was there beside her. Still, the shadow's words chased her into an abyss.

You'll pay. You'll pay with the one you love most.

Light from the window had become hues of sunset when her eyes opened. Pa watched her, a worry line etched between his hairy eyebrows. Like when Mama'd been hurt. She'd tried to climb into bed beside her with her squirmy eight-year-old body. Pa'd hoisted her with one arm up off the bed, whacked her behind, and hauled her into the hallway.

He'd shouted at her. "Don't you know? Don't you care? Silly-ass kid."

After that day, Missy'd tried to be quiet and not a bother. But all that trying hadn't helped. Grief had clung to their days like cheap plastic wrap, sticking where it didn't belong, not sticking where it should have.

After Mama died, Missy had fled to the sycamore tree by the river. Its limbs were reflected in the earthy brown water she'd loved. No crystal blue waters here. Not like the mountain stream she'd seen in the Smokies, cleansed by rocks and pebbles as it cascaded through foaming rapids into quiet pools.

This was her river, smack-dab in the middle of Mississippi. Unpredictable and unsafe, it stank when rain stirred its thick sludge of mud beneath brown pebbles and river stones. Its currents were hidden, dangerous to those foolish enough to jump into those waters without so much as a limb tossed in to discover what couldn't be seen.

She'd done her best to understand. To find that limb and toss it into unknown waters. Once again, it had been too late. And not enough.

Chapter 3

She'd had to stay at the hospital overnight. Doc said she was dehydrated and suffering from exhaustion. No kidding. Fear chased her like a charging bull. It trampled her dreams and rested like a lead pipe on her chest day and night.

She couldn't move. Couldn't run. Couldn't do anything except wait. Wait for him to appear, like she knew he would. It was his voice she heard in every corner of her thoughts. He'd make her pay if she told anyone.

He'd make her pay with Pa.

Missy didn't have strength to go back to the river. Pa hadn't said anything about his knife. She'd go back later. Maybe.

She slept, ate a little, then slept again at home in her own bed. Day merged into another night and a hazy stew of images as she shifted in and out of consciousness.

Random events came to her mind in perfect detail, as if she was reliving them there in her bedroom. Like the time she hadn't recognized a river's current. And it'd almost killed her.

Pa'd had business in Woodville that June morning, so Missy tagged along. He'd gone into the feed store, found a buddy, and started drinking coffee. They talked farm reports and politics around an old whiskey barrel filled with peanuts. Missy figured they'd be growin' roots before they got done, so she went for a walk.

The Homochitto River flowed into the Mississippi nearby. She'd watched a surface current curl around a granite cliff. Flecks of mica and quartz glittered in the sunlight, the rock extending far into the river's depths.

Missy had stuck her foot in to test the current. It was cool. Too cool for snakes. It seemed calm enough. Slipping off her shoes, she'd jumped in. The cold water startled her. Then the main current, hidden below the surface, yanked her down to the base of the cliff.

She'd tried to swim forward, but the current hurtled her body into the deep. Lungs aching, she fought panic, then yielded. Inky black turned into murky light as the same current that had pulled her down shot her upward into the shallows.

Crawling onto the bank, she panted with huge gasps. The river had its rules. Just had to know them.

Felt like that current was sucking her down right now.

Long before she was ready, she and Pa jolted with the ruts of country back roads on their way to Ephraim's funeral. Her face burned and sweat dripped down her back as she peered over cotton fields. Rains had come at the worst time, saturating once creamy white tufts with streaks of red clay. Bad news for farmers.

The river snaked nearby. Missy closed her eyes, hoping daylight would keep the memory buried. It didn't.

Pa turned where a white-framed church stood waiting by the road. Parked cars were scattered on the church grounds under shade trees. Reverend Campbell greeted them as they walked into the flutter of fans waved by perspiring mourners.

It was the Second Baptist Church. Missy guessed the title of First Baptist belonged to white parishioners. Ephraim had told her once that this had been his church since he was a little boy. He told her how the congregation used to repeat each line of a song after the worship leader. Not many could read in those days.

Unlike Ephraim, who devoured books and shared them with whoever was willing to listen to his long-winded reviews. For the most part, he was loved in their small town. Even though the newspaper hinted that his murder had been about racism, white man against black, she didn't believe it. She wasn't sure anyone else did, either.

Ephraim had been an attorney. He was born and raised in Avalon but finished law school and started his practice in Jackson. His wife had died long ago, but his daughter, Mary Beth, and her family still lived in town.

He'd had lots of reasons to come back home often. For one thing, he and Jeremiah Lucas had founded the local shelter for teenage girls. There'd been a string of runaways in the last few years. The shelter was an attempt to keep the girls safe when their homes weren't.

Some folks around town still hated blacks. But Ephraim crossed over all kinds of barriers. He wasn't one of those bleeding-heart people whose sweetness made you sick. Like making the right appearance was all that mattered. He was more like a bridge over troubled waters. Seemed to carry peace no matter where he went.

If Missy'd needed an attorney, like now, she would've hired Ephraim. Except it was her turn to stand for what was right.

And she'd decided not to.

Nobody ever talked about the cost of doing the right thing. Like a price on a fine piece of jewelry she'd never be able to afford or a truck that didn't sputter before it started, doing the right thing was an investment in hoping that the cost mattered. That it'd make a difference.

Missy'd already decided. Nothing was worth risking Pa for.

Nothing.

Large white hats bobbed like a flock of egrets. Amens filled the sanctuary. Mary Beth, Ephraim's daughter, sat on the front row. Missy pulled on a strand of hair hanging over one ear, resisting the urge to stick it in her mouth. Her nose itched, and she sneezed. It didn't seem like time for normal things, like blowing her nose.

She looked around the church. There were a few white faces. Sheriff Emmett Davis sat with his wife, Lou Ann. He caught her staring and nodded. Missy jerked her gaze to the other side of the room. Jimmy Collins, who managed the Motel Six right off the highway, sat near the front. Merle Owen, who owned the local Rexall Drug Store, sat behind him.

Who'd been in that mob that killed Ephraim? Had they all been white? Missy hadn't been able to tell. It had been too dark, and besides, angry voices were color blind. She hadn't been able to make out what they were saying.

It didn't matter. Rage had its own voice.

She and Pa sat behind the pew where Miss Emily Bartow and her sister, Lula May, smiled at her and Pa, nodded, then turned and commenced whispering.

"Poor thing. Death of her mother…sad. So sad."

Was she invisible? They must think she was deaf, too. Nosy old bats. *Death of her mother*. Sounded like a back-page article in the *Avalon Gazette*. Mama, who'd smelled like warm cinnamon on milk toast pulled out of the oven on a cold winter morning. Mama, who'd sung to Pa until his ears turned red.

The tire swing still hung from the gnarled oak in the front yard. They'd pushed and pumped, legs entwined, until soft leaves brushed their faces in the branches above. The empty place Mama left groaned inside her today.

She remembered the day they'd watched an eagle soar in the hills that surrounded the river.

"Never know when a storm is comin'," Mama'd said. "But eagles do. They fly to the highest peak, then wait as the winds build. At just the right time, the storm shoots them straight up, above it." Missy could almost hear her voice. "Don't fear the storm, Missy. Let its winds take you up to a new place. It's there, waitin' for you."

She wondered about that high place. The winds sure were blowin'. Only now, there wasn't a safe one in sight. No matter how high she climbed.

Missy remembered the day she'd met Ephraim. She'd hopped on her bike and headed through town. Pa'd been in a funk, school'd been a pain, and nothing felt right except jumping on her bike and riding. Patched tires thumped over sidewalks and jolted her behind.

Lowering her head, she'd mowed forward. A red Schwinn came from behind a parked car and braked in front of her. It'd been too late to swerve. Metal and bike tires collided with shins and tennis shoes. Missy had fallen off her bike, but not before her toe got caught in the chain. She wrenched her ankle.

"Ow, ow, ow!" She lay on the soft grass of someone's front yard. Benjamin Eckstein lay sprawled out beside her. Blood trickled from a gash on his forehead, more from one on his left shin.

If she wondered how things could get worse, worse had shown up in Clarence Lucas, Jeremiah's son. He'd walked toward them with an ugly laugh.

"Looks like you two had a little accident. And right in my front yard." Clarence hulked overhead. "Bleeding on my grass. Why, that can't be legal."

He pulled his boot back to kick Benjamin. Missy reached up and caught it. He yanked it away and laughed. "Lover boy, huh?"

Missy'd looked into his eyes, slit into a jeer. He drew the boot forward until it rested on her left cheekbone.

"Could rearrange that face, couldn't I? One good kick and your nose'd decorate those freckles in a whole new way. No big loss. Ugly can't get much uglier."

"Now, what would make you say that about such a pretty face?"

Missy turned her head to see who was talking. The voice had come from a tall black man standing nearby. Something in his quiet dignity had shifted the atmosphere.

Clarence had looked confused, then turned ugly.

"When did you get back in town, Ephraim? And what would you do about it, if I did put my boot in the middle of those orange freckles?"

"Clarence, your daddy and I go way back. Besides, it's not what *I* would do." Ephraim pointed to a black-and-white squad car pulling up along the curb. "It's what *he* would do."

Clarence stepped backwards and tripped on a potted begonia before righting himself and loping inside his front door. A damask curtain fluttered as the door slammed.

The man stepped closer. "My name is Ephraim Moriah. May I say you handled yourself with courage? Kudos to you."

Heat rose to her face as he'd helped her to her feet. Then, Ephraim knelt and placed a clean handkerchief on Benjamin's shin.

"Thanks, Mr. Moriah." Benjamin leaned forward and extended his hand to Ephraim.

"Doesn't your mama run the Red Currant Inn?" Ephraim asked. "The one that pulls all those Yankees here to Avalon? Heard her biscuits make orange marmalade jealous. Fine hospitality, indeed."

Benjamin smiled and nodded.

"Yer lookin' mighty rough, girl." Sheriff Davis stood in front of Missy. His jowls flapped as he frowned, making him look like an ancient blood hound.

"You finish up here, Sheriff, and I'll get these two kids home," said Ephraim.

"That'd be a help, thanks."

Ephraim had taught her about kindness without even trying. She'd watched him stop, look a person in the eye, and listen. Really listen. They'd fished together with the grandkids and had even had a few whittlin' contests. Each time Ephraim returned to his law practice in Jackson, Missy knew he'd be back.

She'd asked him why he'd shown up that morning out of nowhere. He said he made it a habit of being in the right place at the right time.

Until one night at the river.

Chapter 4

It was Pa's *What the hell* voice she heard first thing the next morning. Along with a string of curses he saved for supreme aggravation.

The early morning fog in her brain cleared in an instant, and she bounded out of bed. It was the bucket of nails she'd placed over the back door. The one she'd meant to dismantle before Pa came in from the garden.

She'd assaulted her dad. The one, she noticed as she came down the stairs, who'd already set a bowl of oatmeal by her seat at the table. Who stood now, blood streaming down his head with fury in his eyes.

Pa's voice raised a few decibels when he saw her walk into the kitchen.

"A bucket of nails over the door?" He dabbed blood dripping down one side of his forehead with a sweat-stained handkerchief. Another puncture wound colored a streak of gray hair. More blood dribbled around the back of his neck.

This was worse than when she'd sawed a porch step and he'd fallen through. He'd twisted his ankle that time and cussed up a storm. But there hadn't been any blood.

"Sorry."

"Sorry for setting a passel of nails to rain on my head?"

"Didn't think you'd come in that door. Anyway,

read about it in *American Survival Guide*." Missy lowered her head. Statistics and factual evidence might work in her favor. At least a little. "Said diversionary tactics scared away potential assailants."

"Assailants? In Avalon?"

Missy bowed her head. She couldn't tell him why everything in her had escalated into high alert.

"You can worry the horns off a billy goat, but do you know where you left your English book? Or that fishing pole I loaned you the other day?"

He had her there. No matter how hard Missy tried, things had a way of detaching from her person and coming to rest in some unknown place. Like his knife.

She didn't have the courage to go back to the river. Not anymore. She'd have to figure out another way to get it back.

He held her shoulders and looked into her eyes, his face a mix of frustration and compassion. "Know this is a hard time, squirt. Just don't gather sticks for bridges you ain't never gonna cross."

"Yessir." Missy hurried to gather the nails on the floor and stuffed them into a nearby pail while he walked toward the bathroom to wash blood out of his hair. She watched a tiny slump appear on the back of his shoulders.

He'd have a long day at the mill and didn't need to be worrying about booby-traps and such. She'd take down that hoe she'd propped above the shed door. And remove the trip line outside the back gate. And dismantle the swinging log trap at the far end of their property.

Tomorrow.

She heard a car pull into the driveway and

stretched her neck over the kitchen window to see Emmett's squad car. She heard his boots stomp across the wooden porch, and knock rattle the screen door.

Pa ambled through the living room with small strips of white adhesive tape scattered on his head, peeking through sandy hair. He opened the door and motioned Emmett inside.

"Emmett."

"Hal. How are ya?"

"Good." It was Pa's *not letting you in* voice. Missy stood beside him. This didn't look right, but maybe he was making a courtesy call to check on her.

The sheriff fumbled in his jacket pocket and pulled something out in a small plastic sack.

She looked closer, hoping she wasn't seeing what she was seeing. It was Pa's knife. Missy sucked in a gasp of air. Sheriff Davis shifted his eyes like a laser beam to hers.

"We found something at the warehouse. Recognize this? It's got your initials on it."

"My knife."

"It was me," said Missy. "Not Pa. I was using it to…for whittling." Her words tumbled out in a babbling stream flowing over a rocky riverbed. It didn't matter if they made sense. Where they coming out fast enough to prove her guilt? And his innocence?

"You left your dad's knife at the warehouse? When?"

Why was Pa's knife in the warehouse? She'd left it at the base of a tree close to the river. Where would she start if she tried to explain? The best place right now was a lie.

"I'd been whittling," she said, taking a gulp of air,

then feeling a belch rise up out of her belly. "Was working on a piece for the fair. Guess I left it there." She couldn't keep the frantic tone out of her voice, no matter how hard she tried.

"Funny how it showed up with dried blood on the blade," said the sheriff

"But that's where I whittle," said Missy. "That's where I sit." Like she'd ever sit in the warehouse to whittle.

"Cut yourself the last time you had it?" Emmett's elbows rested on his knees as he studied Missy's face.

"No. I mean, yes. I don't remember."

The sheriff shifted his attention to Pa. "You and Ephraim ever have words, Hal? Any kind of argument?"

"You know we didn't. I barely knew him."

"Except for that one time." Sheriff Davis arched his brows and shot Pa a knowing look. Pa glared back, arms tight against his sides and fists clenched.

"That was a long time ago. We settled it, and it was over."

"Except maybe it wasn't." It was clear the sheriff had an agenda and wasn't ready to let it go. Regardless of Pa's resistance, which had moved from irritation to confrontation.

"What are you trying to say?" Pa's tone demanded an answer. Sheriff Davis shifted his eyes from Pa and backed down a few degrees. Then straightened his shoulders and kept going.

"It's been a few years ago, but…"

"Few years. It's been five, at least," said Pa, as if he answered an obvious question that both of them knew the answer to. "A labor dispute at the mill. No big deal."

"Okay. But Ephraim won that case for management. Union lost. You two fought. Got ugly. Your job…"

The back of Pa's ears had turned scarlet. It was the sign his body made when he'd controlled himself long enough and was about to blow. He looked over at Missy, then back to Emmett. "Do you mind?"

Emmett cleared his throat. "Can't be helped, Hal. I gotta have answers. Either here or down at the station. Would rather talk here."

"My pa wasn't there that night."

Emmett looked up in surprise. "How do you know?"

"Because I know. I mean, I just know. He was here, with me."

"But it was early morning, dark. How would you have known?"

Missy paced back and forth, yanking a tangled curl straight again and again. Her voice rose into a cry. "I know… I know he wasn't there."

"No need to get riled up. Hal, I'll be back in touch."

Sheriff Davis turned and walked away, letting the screen door slam behind him.

A tidal wave of shame rushed through her and spilled out in small words of helpless regret. "I left your knife at the river."

"Tell me. Now." Pa crossed his arms and gave her that I'm-not-kidding look she'd seen so often. "Everything you saw."

Missy gulped. "I was…It was raining. In the middle of the night. But I remembered I'd left your knife by a tree at the river. I ran down to find it and bring it home."

"In the middle of the night? What were you thinking?" Pa looked at her like he'd never seen her before. She'd lied to him and suddenly this wasn't about the knife anymore.

"Guess I wasn't." Missy lowered her head and couldn't look in his eyes.

"Go on," he said. There was hardness in his voice. And something else. Missy searched around the perimeter of everything she knew about her dad. Then found it. He'd been like that after Mama died. Refused to cry, turned his back when he thought Missy'd read his face. It was hurt and fear all mixed up in one ugly heap.

A new kind of terror stirred inside her. He was disappointed in her. He'd trusted her, and she'd let him down.

"I got close to the warehouse. There were some men. I think men. They were around this body. Ephraim's."

"You saw the murder?" Pa pulled his hand over his brow, as if to stop sweat from pouring into his eyes. Only it wasn't hot. An early winter had blown in a chill that moved from the windows and throughout the family room. They stood at the front door, even though Sheriff Davis was long gone. Maybe because they knew somehow home would never be the same.

"Don't know, 'cept they were kicking him, stabbing. I…"

"What'd you do?"

"I hid behind some trash barrels. Rain let up, and I went to see who it was. I saw a man. He'd been there.

"I was…I could've…"

Pa stood looking at her with that question in his gaze. He didn't hold out his arm to hug her. If only he would. Maybe the tension in the air would filter out the front door like the gust that had blown in with Sheriff Davis.

Everything in her longed to start over. To change her mind about that run to the river. Not only because of what she'd seen and couldn't forget. But for what she saw in her dad's eyes.

"Why didn't you tell me?" There it was, thought Missy. They could've worked things out together. Like always. At least until now.

"I was chicken," she said, knowing that any honesty at this point was too little and too late.

Pa stood frozen in place. Missy wished she could read his mind, so she could rush in and explain what possessed her to mess things up so bad. Not that she understood herself. Besides, his head tracked realities she didn't know anything about. That's because he always made sure she was safe. Whether she knew it or not.

Leaving that knife implicated her dad in a murder, and now the word *sorry* was too weak to matter. Nothing she could think of was strong enough to keep them both from heading into the rapids.

That night the house was alive with creaks and groans, even though no breeze stirred in the branches outside her window. Fear grabbed her belly with each sound. But it was the threat behind all those noises that squeezed her like a vise.

Missy remembered the meals Pa'd made after Mama was gone. How terrible they were. And how he'd tucked her under his strong arm to read adventures of a silly monkey, even though he was tired after a long day at work.

They'd moved into a routine, and she'd felt comfort even though she understood now that Pa still hurt. He'd held it together for her. Only now even he wasn't able to keep her world from falling apart.

Worse, she had to go to school in the morning. Pa'd given her some time off, but that night he laid down the law.

"Want to repeat the eighth grade?"

"Umm, no."

The thought of school made her belly flip in greater flops than it already did. Back to school right now was more like backed into a corner with no way out. Everyone in town knew about Ephraim's murder. It'd been announced on TV, blared on front page headlines in the *Avalon Gazette*, and the subject of coffee shop conversations. People in Avalon still leaned over their hedges to share their opinions about the days' events. Missy knew she'd been the subject in more than a few of those discussions.

But school was another beast all together. Pa was pretty ticked that her name was in the paper as the one who discovered Ephraim's body, being a minor and all. But the newspaper didn't see it that way.

Adults nodded at her, a few pulled her aside to give her a hug. But kids? Who knew?

She hated being in the spotlight. Especially not being able to control how she reacted to what hurt beyond words. Would she be humiliated again for being somewhere she hadn't planned to be—and seeing what she hadn't meant to see? Or maybe the man who'd threatened her had planted spies at school.

Then there was Clarence Lucas. Just weeks ago, when her English teacher had called her up to the desk, he'd extended his muddy boot in time to hurl her into a sprawling face plant in front of the whole class. Her nose had ached for a week and the unfortunate meeting with that boot had dashed any hopes for rising above loser status.

A sparrow sounded his musical trill outside her window. She remembered what Mama'd said about birds singing early in the morning. Their songs were proof they'd made it through the night. Proof that they were still strong enough to face a new day. She wasn't much of a singer, but without any other choice, she guessed she'd show up and survive whatever came next.

Miss Terrell had assigned oral reports a couple weeks ago. Ones, according to her preassignment pep talk, that were vital to their future success. An assignment she'd ignored and hoped would somehow go away.

Standing in front of a bunch of preadolescent dweebs was going to matter for her adult life? Teachers invented those assignments to torture kids. The last time she had to speak in front of the class, her body took on a life of its own, cheeks twitching and sweat traveling down her forehead and into her eyes. Even her heart betrayed her, pounding as she tugged on her T-shirt for a breath of air.

She hauled butt to school the next morning, as close to the tardy bell as she could. Fewer words, fewer reactions that way. The oral reports were right up there in the middle of all her dread. She sat stone-faced in class, waiting like gallows beckoned.

Miss Terrell turned to Benjamin. "Are you ready to share your report?"

He looked startled, wiped his hands on his khakis, and answered, "Yeah."

Missy looked at Miss Terrell in alarm. She hated to think what Pa'd do if she answered a grown-up that way. He'd raised her from the cradle with "yes, ma'am" and "no, sir." It was the *slap you silly* threat made good that helped her remember. Any kid in the South who didn't address an adult by "ma'am" or "sir" was an uncouth heathen... She'd just say it. *Yankee.*

It was law, no matter how vile or kind the adult was. Benjamin and his family broke lots of Southern rules. For one thing, they were Jewish, not Baptist or Methodist. Truth be told, she and Pa only showed up at church twice a year, whether they needed it or not.

It was during one of those rare visits she'd about gotten herself booted out of Sunday school. She'd noticed a picture of Jesus fixed to a pale green concrete wall. His blonde hair flowed in perfect waves around the shoulders of a soft blue robe. Clean, happy children surrounded Him. With a sudden burst of curiosity, she asked if Jesus had been raised up North.

A horrified look from the teacher, Twila Lee's mother, proved it was the wrong question at the wrong time. How would she know? The picture made Jesus look like He might keel over in a sudden gust or that He'd never known southern heat in August. And blue eyes? Benjamin's eyes were so dark they looked black under the long bangs that shielded them.

Missy watched as he straightened his shoulders, grabbed a stack of papers, and headed to the front.

Benjamin was pretty skittish as a rule. The KKK had firebombed his granddaddy's house years ago. They didn't cotton to the fact the Ecksteins, transplants from New York City, chose to live where they weren't wanted. His granddaddy had been burned badly and died later that night.

Some things had changed, but people still didn't trust different. Hated change no matter how loud they sang in the choir on Sunday morning. Jesus-loving or not.

"My topic today is catapults," he said, balancing on one leg like a stork. The class tittered among themselves but perked up. Missy heard his voice go from quivering voice to a nerdy enthusiasm.

"A catapult is a mechanism designed to launch a projectile a great distance without explosives or machines." He held up a diagram from the *Encyclopedia Britannica.*

"Ancient Greeks invented it to increase the range of their arrows. In the Middle Ages, when most cities were protected by massive walls, enemy armies used catapults to toss fiery missiles over the walls."

His eyes lit up. "Sometimes, they even used a kind of biological warfare, catapulting garbage and dead, rotting animals into the city. I used a model of a medieval catapult to build one in my garage. Here's the blueprint. It sails things through the air. Just for fun."

"Cool," someone whispered.

"Can I try it?" asked another. It didn't take long for pandemonium to break out in the class.

"Settle down, class. Let him finish," Miss Terrell said.

"Still working out some flaws," said Benjamin.

"Should be ready to try out in a few weeks."

"Amazing presentation. We'll look forward to a demonstration," said Miss Terrell.

"Loser," Clarence Lucas muttered as Benjamin walked back to his seat.

After class, Benjamin stood outside the door and fell into step with her as she walked into the hallway.

"Hey," he said.

Missy turned, confused. Was he talking to her?

"Well, I…" Benjamin stammered, then blurted out, "I heard you were at the river, saw Ephraim. I'm sorry."

Missy looked down at the green linoleum tile. "Thanks."

"I liked Ephraim. A lot. He…Would you…? I mean, you can come over and see the catapult, if you want."

Missy looked at him as if he'd invited her to watch a neighborhood dog fight.

Benjamin blushed. "Sorry, I mean…"

The last thing Missy wanted to do was check out a catapult. But when she looked into his eyes, she saw her own. Trying to reach out, but afraid. Benjamin was the only one who'd cared to notice what she'd seen at the river. Cared that it might hurt.

She nodded her head, turned, and ran into a locker.

Chapter 5

Missy stood at the giant oak door of Benjamin's house at four o'clock. Lord knew what kind of meeting this would be. Benjamin was about as social as she was. Even though they'd been in school together for a while, they hadn't hung out. She'd never been inside his house, which was more like a mansion.

Rubbing away sweat, Missy tucked her T-shirt into jean shorts. Benjamin opened the front door and greeted her like a British butler, bowing as he motioned her inside. Then he turned back inside to answer a shrill voice.

"Benjamin! Come. Here. Now."

Missy wondered if shouting in a series of commands was a Yankee form of communication. Southern convention required a certain amount of polite banter before getting to the point. In front of company, anyway.

He held his hand up. "Give me a minute. I'll be right back."

Mrs. Eckstein's voice rose through the partly opened front door, strained and angry. Already Missy felt like an unwelcome guest showing up uninvited for dinner right at six o'clock. She had a feeling this would only get worse.

"Your shoes are muddy. Get them off. Guests are coming in two hours."

"They're not muddy, but whatever."

"And your shirt. What did you dribble down yourself today?"

"Mom. It was ketchup. No big deal."

Missy shuddered. This was only going downhill fast. And here she was at the front door, listening in on a conversation not meant for her ears. She wanted to run back home and forget she'd come to visit.

"It *is* a big deal. You look like one of those crackers who…"

"I know. One of those *dumber than a rock* Southerners."

"Don't talk back to me."

"They aren't all stupid, Mom."

Missy made a mental note of Mrs. Eckstein's opinion of Southerners. She and Pa could check off an invitation to Sunday dinner.

"That. Is. Enough."

"How can you put on the gracious bed-and-breakfast act every day?"

"I said, enough." Mrs. Eckstein had dismissed her son. A good time to exit herself. She heard the final command as she started walking down the front steps. "Go upstairs and change. Now."

It was quiet for a minute, and Missy paused on the steps. Benjamin spoke again.

"Missy Needham's outside. Can she come in for a minute?"

Silence. No quick exit now. She was toast.

"You didn't tell me someone was here."

Mrs. Eckstein opened the door. Missy cringed and turned to look back at a woman who looked like Jackie Kennedy, complete with cream-colored linen dress and black flats. She sized up Missy in one long glance, stained tennies and all.

Looking for a crack in the veneer of her porcelain skin, Missy found only contempt beneath the courteous nod.

"Hello, dear. Come in. Excuse the mess, I'm preparing for guests."

"Don't worry," Benjamin whispered as he led the way across the tiled foyer into the kitchen. "Mom's been teaching me history for years. Hitler, KKK, white crackers—you know, hoping some kind of pain will stick."

Pain'd have a hard time attaching to Benjamin. She'd watched him come and go at school. He didn't appear to be moved by his social outcast status and seemed pretty happy most the time. As far as she could tell he wasn't the kind who held much of a grudge. Forget eons of injustice. Like her, he was probably just trying to survive eighth grade.

The scents of vanilla and brown sugar drifted down a massive hallway. They followed Mrs. Eckstein into the kitchen where golden oak cabinets rose up to ten-foot ceilings. Bronze tile set a soft glow over black counters. A weathered oak plank table fit into the alcove with windows that extended from floor to ceiling.

"We're working on an assignment," said Benjamin. He directed it to his mom as they waited together for directions. No invitation to sit down and have a cookie, none of the typical mom responses after a long day at school.

"Really?" Her voice rose along with her eyebrows. Those were pretty impressive eyebrows. Missy's after-school belly growled as she watched his mom pull a tray of chocolate chip cookies from the oven. She angled a spatula to place each cookie in perfect rows on the cooling rack, then glanced up at Benjamin.

"What kind of project?" She wiped her hands as if the inconvenience of a pause in her work was more than she could bear. Missy's stomach growled again. Mrs. Eckstein moved the racks of cookies to another counter.

"Science." Benjamin nodded toward the back door and led the way out into a large garage. So much for an afternoon snack, Missy thought as she glanced back at the cookies.

She examined the lumber structure extending to the garage's roof. It looked like a medieval torture device, with a spring-loaded catapult and a basket ready to launch its contents across the nearest moat. "This thing is bigger than my house."

Benjamin walked around it with the pride of a master craftsman, describing the physics behind its mechanism. He paused when he looked at her face—no doubt a blank stare, since she had no idea what he was talking about.

"Made it with lumber from the mill," he said. Apparently, he could give her a dumbed-down version. "Here's the trip lever." He pointed to a piece of wood that looked just like the rest. "You put a basket on top. Too bad we don't have any walled cities to throw dead coons over. Anyway, what's your plan?"

"What plan?"

"Look, I don't know what it was like to see…to see Ephraim at the river. Must have been…Anyway, there's one enemy we can handle. When the time comes, I'm in," he said.

"In what?"

"There has to be a way to defeat him."

"Him?"

"You know. Clarence."

Her mind had been a long way from Clarence. He'd been the source of most of her misery at school for years. But now with Ephraim's murder, he didn't seem important anymore. Everything in school had dimmed to a filtered light that reminded her that nothing was the same. Anywhere.

"I can't. I…just can't. Sorry."

"That's okay. Wanted you to…you know…I'm here to help. So to speak." He blushed through his black curls that kept popping out despite every attempt to slick them down.

Awkward. That's what it was. Missy tried to smile back, but nothing in her face cooperated. She turned away and bolted down the long driveway, not looking back until she got home.

The next morning Missy was headed to class when she saw Clarence shove Benjamin into a line of metal lockers. Clarence's large hand hovered over Benjamin like a lion's paw, gripping his shoulder and slamming him into the nearest locker. A fine line of blood trickled down Benjamin's neck from one ear. A few kids ducked and ran, except for the ones who hoped to watch a good fight.

"You worthless, low-life beast," Missy said, eyes locked on Clarence's.

"One goon down," said Clarence. "One more to go."

He slouched away before Miss Terrell saw him. The young teacher rushed to Benjamin and sent the nearest onlooker to get paper towels. She grabbed a tissue out of her sleeve and held it against his ear, then looked up to a wispy sixth-grader.

"Find Mr. Wintroble," she said. Then she turned to the rest of the crowd. "Who did this?"

Benjamin wouldn't look at her. "Nobody. Just fell," he mumbled to the floor.

"Fell? That is not what happened. I demand to know who did this."

"I'm fine."

"It was Clarence," said Missy. "He smashed Benjamin's head against the locker."

Mr. Wintroble, the school counselor, ambled around the corner of the hallway. He was a large man in a sweat-stained collared shirt. Missy wasn't sure what his job was because he did his best to stay as far from kids as he could. She imagined him in his office with the door locked, eating cookies his wife sent in a brown paper bag. From the looks of his belly, he'd polished off more than a few sacks.

He had a strange way about him. He seemed nice but in a creepy sort of way. Missy had gone in to see him last year when grades had come out for the new middle schoolers. Hers were so bad they warranted a special time with the counselor. Mr. Wintroble had shown her random pictures and asked her how they made her feel.

Sick. That's how she'd felt. But she sure wasn't telling him. Not then. Not now.

Miss Terrell interrupted. "I found Benjamin on the floor after Clarence Lucas attacked him. Missy Needham saw it. Said he slammed Benjamin's head against a locker. He's injured."

"What happened here, Benjamin?"

"Nothin'. Just ran into my locker."

Why wouldn't he tell them it was Clarence? Why would he let that creep get by with this?

"I see. I'll take it from here, Miss Terrell. Don't you worry yourself. He'll be fine."

He smiled and patted Miss Terrell's shoulder. Missy saw the teacher flinch and wondered if she'd slap him. Miss Terrell was young and pretty, but she wasn't stupid. A good slap might just clear the air.

"These things happen," he continued. "No big deal."

"He's bleeding. It doesn't look like an accident to me." Miss Terrell's face flamed and she held her arms tight against the side of her body. Like if she didn't, she'd wallop the man.

"Like I said, I'll handle it. Don't worry your pretty head."

Miss Terrell strode back into her classroom. Missy heard her muttering. "Old buzzard…" She plopped down at her desk and shuffled papers as she tapped her foot in angry staccatos on the tile floor.

Benjamin was quiet the rest of the day. He didn't look up from his desk and watched the floor as he walked. Missy tried to get his attention, but he ignored her.

It wasn't right. Clarence had pounded him and gotten away with it. Nobody did a thing. The scumbag smirked at everyone in class and laughed when Benjamin passed by.

Missy wondered about the mob she'd seen at the river. Had they been bullies growing up? Maybe they'd gotten by with it. Maybe the hallways had cleared when they'd lit into some innocent kid.

What could she do? She hated Clarence. Despised the way he used and abused people. She'd track Benjamin down at his house. After all, he wouldn't want any show of weakness at school. Especially with her being a loser and all. She'd only make him look worse by showing sympathy.

That afternoon, Missy knocked on the giant door and waited. Benjamin answered, then turned away as if he was going to close the door.

"Wait!" Missy started a fast-paced spiel before he could leave. "I watched this show about the Ice Age last night," she said. "Something took down the Neanderthals, right? A saber-tooth tiger, lying in wait. Patient until the giant was unaware, or better, distracted." Without taking a breath, she continued. "With no saber-toothed tigers at hand, maybe we could get some licks in. Not that we're Neanderthals or whatever. Still, we could make him pay."

She quit talking to take a breath. Benjamin perked up but didn't speak.

"Not by one person, but by a team," she added.

Was she calling she and Benjamin a team? A smile played on his lips, and he looked as if he was trying not to look pleased. He picked a tiny fleck of lint off his sweater and combed his hair back with his fingers. A dimple appeared in one cheek as the smile took over.

"What's your plan?"

"Bullies are met best head-on." Like she knew about that. Like she'd ever done anything so brave in her life. Still, she watched the pain lifting from Benjamin's face, so she kept going.

"They don't take a hint. We could stage an

intervention."

"A what?" Benjamin asked.

"You know, teach him a lesson. Help him overcome his sociopath tendencies."

"Sociopath?"

"The kind who doesn't care who he hurts. Wants to inflict pain for no reason except for the twisted joy of seeing someone hurt. What we need is some kind of bait. Some way to draw him into a trap." She thought, then added, "Maybe we could dig one of those jungle pits and fill it with scorpions."

Benjamin scrunched his eyebrows, silent.

Missy rushed in to fill in the quiet place. "Scorpions aren't hard to find around here. Course, Pa wouldn't be happy about a giant hole on our property. Your land is out of the question. Got any ideas?"

"Maybe." Benjamin looked at her as if he'd never seen her. He paused for a long minute. Missy thought she'd lost him by the time he finally spoke up. "We could use the catapult. Or something like it."

"The catapult? On Clarence?"

"We'd have to set something up in the right place. Make sure it's hidden. And use some kind of bait to lure him to it."

"Bait?"

"Yes."

"What kind of bait? Cheeseburgers?"

"No. Better than that."

"Like what?"

"Like you."

Chapter 6

"Me?" Missy shook her head. "For bait?"

"Why not? You're so pretty, he'd follow you anywhere."

Heat rose from her belly and traveled up her cheeks. Benjamin thought she was pretty? Maybe she heard him wrong. Or he was cracking a joke. "Are you serious? He hates me."

"Right. I may not be a Neanderthal, but I know how one thinks. Believe me. You'd be the best bait ever."

"I don't know. I mean, he calls me all kinds of names. Thinks I'm ugly."

"He's a liar. Believe me."

Missy studied Benjamin's intent brown eyes that peered into hers. They didn't waver. He didn't slap his leg, gasp for breath, or grab his stomach as he laughed.

For whatever reason, he was telling the truth.

He thought she was pretty. Even in the old T-shirt she'd pulled off the closet floor when she'd been in a rush that morning. Brushing a stray lock of hair behind one ear, she straightened her shoulders.

Wait a minute. He'd called her bait. What was he thinking?

Benjamin continued, his voice rising with enthusiasm. "Using some aerodynamics, we can snag him in a way he won't forget. And hold him till he gets the picture."

"Where in the heck are you planning to do this?" Missy felt as if a current were pulling her where she had no intention of going.

"We need a place with lots of trees and brush cover. How about the river? I know just the place."

The river. No way. Benjamin didn't understand why that was impossible. Didn't know the fear that still took over her body like a thieving buzzard at the worst times. No way.

Except...she'd helped Pa set traps on the farm. A snare was set up by knowing its prey. When prey was caught, it lunged forward and away. That instinct set the noose tighter. There were a few unknowns, like taking into account an animal's weight. The larger the mass, the greater the propulsion.

"It might work," Missy said. Her gaze lingered on Benjamin's dark eyes.

It didn't take long to sketch out a plan. Not that it was a great one. Benjamin got more excited the longer they talked. Maybe she'd catch some of his courage later.

Bait. She hadn't attracted much except misery lately. Never cared a whole lot about how she looked. Didn't want to stink, of course. She had to admit that climbing out of river water and running home on a summer afternoon wasn't a great combination. The earthy smell of river stayed in her hair when it dried into clumps. Add some sweat and she got pretty stout.

But to shut down Clarence Lucas? Was that even possible? No one else had ever tried. Until Benjamin. What made him so strong? He didn't look like anyone special. But something inside...Then she had a weird thought.

Maybe he was doing this for her.

No. Couldn't be. He was just sick of Clarence in general. Or maybe…

Missy didn't know where to follow that train of thought. Her head had never gone in that direction. No one had ever taken up for her, outside of Pa. Her heart fluttered and she blushed, then turned away so he didn't notice.

For whatever reason, it was kind and brave of him. Maybe they could make a team. Not that she'd contribute much. Except to be bait, according to Benjamin.

What if the plan didn't work? What if Clarence turned it back on them or returned with a vengeance against some other kid? That would be like him.

Missy kept thinking about that mob. How they'd watched, even helped, someone kill an innocent man. Was that the direction Clarence was headed if no one ever kicked back at the pain he dished out?

Afternoon light was still bright on the horizon and its warmth soaked into her skin as she headed downtown. The brick exterior of Rexall Drugs had been there as long as she remembered. *Discount Prescriptions* and *Cigarettes* blazed in bright script across the window.

Missy hadn't cared about anything in the store other than the sweet foam of ice cream floats she slurped as she twirled in the swivel seats at the soda fountain. But now she meandered down the aisles and noticed the magazine section. She picked up one that featured an article called, *How to Pull off the Year's Hottest Trends*. A model's smile promised that anyone, even Missy, could be glossy and gorgeous with only a few strategic steps.

Skinny models with just the right amount of cool were a long way from the skin she lived in. Sighing, she ambled down the cosmetic aisle.

"May I help you?" asked a store clerk.

"No, ma'am, I'm just lookin'."

The lady seemed suspicious. Missy wanted to wave the cash under her nose. She picked out a bottle of light ivory foundation, then moved down to the blush. Cream or powder. How would she know? She picked out a rosy pink in a clear plastic compact. Then she chose a green apple-scented shampoo. Crème rinse, too.

She'd try it out. The clerk nodded her approval as she checked Missy out, probably happy to see some improvements in store for tangled curls and a mass of freckles.

At home, Missy brushed her teeth, washed her face, and smeared on creamy foundation. Amazing. The freckles faded into sprinkles under an ivory background. She looked again and washed it off. Maybe another time.

Heading back to the mirror, she dabbed blush on her cheekbones. Freckles turned muddy red. Washing her face again, she dabbed foundation and a small dot of blush on both cheeks. Maybe no one would notice.

The crème rinse softened her curls. They still stuck out, but not like unruly sprouts of crimson straw. She smoothed the new sky-blue T-shirt she found on the clearance rack. Even the checker said it brought out the blue in her eyes. Finally, she finger-plaited her hair in one long braid down her back.

Time to blaze a trail.

She waited until lunchtime the next day when Clarence was alone, wolfing down a burger with yellow processed cheese. After practicing a smile for hours that morning, she could paste it on in seconds.

Steeling her insides, she pulled up a smile as she got closer. Just a little one at first, then bigger as she remembered the bait.

"Hey, Clarence."

"Hey yourself, zit-face."

"Well, I just…I found something at the river you might be interested in."

Clarence looked up, then back at his burger. "Really. You have something that would interest me?" Obviously, all her work to add make-up and hair products had been for nothing. Clarence was unmoved.

"It's a surprise."

"I don't do surprises, stupid."

"You might if you knew what this one was."

Missy had practiced an enticing look in the mirror. It was hopeless. When she was about to turn away, a tiny interest in Clarence's eyes gave her hope.

"When?" he asked.

"Any time."

"How about tonight. Around dark?"

"You'll need some light to see it. About four?"

"Alrighty then. I'll be there."

Missy smiled again. Maybe she should join the next school drama. She could get an Academy award. Not yet, though.

****

The sun had already started its long descent over the horizon that afternoon. Benjamin had agreed to hide nearby. She and Clarence would meet on the ridge overlooking the deep pool where birch trees stood on each side of the river. Benjamin had shown her right where he'd place the trip wire. She needed to make sure Clarence's foot found that spot.

Benjamin was never late, but he hadn't shown up yet. If he didn't make it soon, Clarence would beat him there. Terror rose up in her throat. She stuffed it back down and made a three-sixty turn, looking in every direction for Benjamin's dark hair and funny gait.

A hawk circled above, and something rustled in the brush. She jumped as a rabbit dove out of the dense cover and took out for the river. Clarence approached the clearing, lumbering toward her. Too late to run now.

Something inside her went into autopilot. Missy waved and moved to the line of trees along the river. She pasted the smile on and moved to a strategic position. Clarence followed. *Just a little closer*.

Clarence stopped. "What's goin' on here?" He looked up and around the area. Missy froze.

"You ain't half bad looking," she said.

Clarence took a giant step toward her, and one of his boots found the snare. The rope triggered and closed around his leg as he lunged forward, determined to get free. Just then, the trip lever hurled a thick branch upward, hauling his body upside down over the river, the other leg flailing.

His head tipped the river as he flew upside down in a giant arc. The limb bowed further. Clarence's eyes were under water with the next arc. He struggled harder, making the cinch tighter.

"You get me down from here. You…" Down went his head.

Clarence pulled his head toward his chest, then

arched backwards. Neither kept his head from skimming through the river's surface. Each gasp followed a glug as his head trailed under water, then popped up on the other side.

Missy's heart pounded. A surge of confidence rose up inside. She'd done it. Clarence would see that he'd been a despicable bully. He'd change. All because of the catapult.

"I want to hear you say sorry." Her voice rang out clear and strong. "Sorry for treatin' everyone like dirt. Heck, I want more than a sorry. I want change. Hear me?"

The pendulum slowed and Clarence's head dangled upside down in the middle of the river. When the swinging came to rest, his mouth and nose were under water.

"Lord, have mercy!" She jumped in and swam to him, straining against the current. When she got there, she extended her arms and pushed his head up just enough to allow him a sputtering gasp of air. She didn't have the strength to keep him there and fight the current that kept dragging her away as Clarence's head went under again.

She wore out fast, trying to stay close and keep his head above water against the unrelenting current. Panic gave her a fresh burst of strength and another idea. Using the river bottom as a launch, she pushed herself up, lifting his head. She did that over and over. The water was deep, though, and it wasn't long till her limbs became mushy and her muscles ached.

The branch kept bobbing Clarence lower into the river.

She hadn't meant to murder him. Just give him a

lesson he wouldn't forget. She thought about Pa and how he'd feel when the newspapers tried to figure out how two teenagers drowned in the river. Clarence upside down and Missy at the bottom, lungs full of mud.

No, sir. That couldn't happen. She lurched up one more time and shoved Clarence's head above water. He gasped and went under again.

A shot rang through the woods. The branch cracked apart, then plummeted Clarence on top of her.

They both plunged under water. Missy tasted the grit of river bottom in her teeth and felt its earthy smell overwhelm her. When the limb rammed into her leg, she grabbed and yanked it as hard as she could. It broke free from Clarence's ankle and drifted away in the current.

They surfaced together, both sputtering and gasping for air out of the river's muddy haze. Pa swam toward them and pulled Clarence to the shore in the crook of one arm. Missy extended her arms in a long breaststroke, angling through the current and crawled to the sandy beach.

Vomiting mud and river water, she turned her head to see Pa flip Clarence on his belly. He worked a deep rolling massage on his back until river muck rolled out of the side of his mouth and Clarence coughed in huge, quaking spasms.

Still on her belly, Missy looked across her vomit to his. Clarence's eyes were wild with fear. But he was alive.

"Thank you, Jesus," she sobbed, then threw up some more. Clarence was alive, no thanks to her. She heaved again, then cried more with relief. Even though this meant he'd try to kill her as soon as he was back to normal.

Pa turned to look at Missy. "Time to call it a night."

"Yes, sir."

She trudged toward home as Pa helped Clarence to his feet. A soft peach glow lined the horizon behind the house and Ranger loped over to give her a slobbery greeting.

"Stay, Ranger." She rubbed his head but kept walking up the porch steps, too tired to play.

Muscles in her legs quivered as she slipped off wet shoes on the porch. The living room was dim, but she didn't switch on any lights. Instead, she crept up the stairs to her bedroom. Her wet clothes were cold and the grit of river silt itched as it dried. She longed for a shower.

Pa'd be coming in shortly and she'd best be ready. For what, she wasn't sure.

Finally, the front screen door slammed. Pa's boots tromped on the wood floors through the living room and up the stairs. She sat straight up on the edge of the bed with hands folded in her lap. The bedroom door creaked as it opened.

Pa stood at the door, holding the frame on both sides as if the walls might fall apart without his support. He stood, staring at Missy with an odd mix of confusion, fear and utmost irritation.

This was bad. No yelling. No threats. A least not yet.

Would she be grounded for life? She steeled herself and kept her gaze on his.

When he spoke, his words were slow and

measured, except for the smoldering wrath that hovered underneath them.

"Don't know what that was back there."

He began like a cold engine struggling to crank, then picked up speed and volume.

"Don't know what kind of shenanigans you were up to or what genius built that gol-darned contraption.

"But I can tell you one thing." He punctuated the *one thing* by stabbing his forefinger in her direction.

"Better not happen again." His finger slashed through the air once more. "Ever."

Pulling in a deep breath, he paused and let it out in a big huff. "Hear me?"

Missy nodded. "Yes, sir."

"Get some sleep. You've got school in the morning." His shoulders slumped as though exhausted and he walked out the door.

Missy expected to feel relief as he disappeared. Instead, guilt pressed against her chest. River grit had tightened on her skin with a ruddy pucker and earthy stench. She didn't have the nerve to face Pa again on the way to the shower downstairs. But left-over stink and regret of this day over-rode her fear.

Grabbing a clean nightgown and underwear, she snuck down the steps and slipped into the bathroom. Warm water from the shower coursed over her aching body. Missy wished the memory of the whole river catastrophe would go down the drain along with the cascading stream. Not likely, though.

The pile of silt-filled clothes lay in a heap on the floor. They'd be stinking bad by morning. She wanted to toss them out the window, but figured that wouldn't go over well with Pa.

Drying off, she got dressed and held the wet clothes in one hand as she crept back up the stairs, taking two at time. She threw the wet clothes in one corner of her room and climbed into bed, then wrapped a threadbare sweater around her shoulders, punched her pillow into the right-sized lump, and fell sound asleep.

Her eyes opened the next morning to sunlight flooding her room. A whiff of river water woke her with a start. She remembered the snare. And how it'd worked so well she'd about murdered Clarence.

The thought about what had almost happened sank to her belly and raced around in fear. What had she been thinking? What if he'd died?

It would've been her fault. All because she was trying to get him back for meanness.

Who was the bully now?

She of all people should've thought about how quickly someone could be lost. To wake up one morning to laughter and search for it later in the silence. The sadness of losing Mama still hit like an unexpected gust, threatening to topple her when she least expected it. Like when she smelled warm yeast rolls in the school cafeteria or saw a mother comforting her little one.

The sweater wrapped around her torso by morning was Mama's. Missy'd found it one day pressed against the back of a drawer in Pa's room. She pretended it was Mama's embrace when darkness fell and she was all alone.

Life right now was a muddy mess of quicksand and Missy didn't know how to stay out of its grasp. Or how to keep anyone else out, for that matter.

She heard Pa already up, putzing around the kitchen. He'd know if she skipped school. Besides, they'd had that little talk last night. Knowing Pa, he'd want her to face any fallout head on.

What a time to be virtuous. It'd be a lot easier to skip school, move to a new town, or even try astral projection into another age. She'd do anything to avoid facing Clarence Lucas.

Missy wondered how he'd make her pay. Would he try something sneaky or just bust her chops in front of everybody? He sure wouldn't slink around the halls. True, she'd blasted him in a big way, but no one had seen it. He could tell the story however he wanted to.

She'd watched Pa drag him to the shore and work the Heimlich on his belly as muddy water and bile spewed out. Gross. But better than pulling a dead Clarence to the shore and Missy headed to prison for the rest of her life.

Payback had had mixed results, for sure. Missy wasn't sure how change worked. Maybe when pain got real bad, some kind of chemical reaction took place in the gut and traveled to the head. People she knew never really changed. Her, most of all.

One glance at the clock told her she had just enough time to get dressed and run to school. She'd arrive at the last minute and hope that being with a teacher (even if it *was* Miss Terrell) would keep Clarence from dishing out immediate retribution.

She dashed in through the front door at school, then searched the perimeter for his hulking shadow. The coast seemed clear.

Except for Benjamin who darted from one hallway toward their home room. She tracked him down, short of pinning him to one wall. Jabbing his chest with one finger, she peppered him with questions.

"So, where were you? No word, no nothin'? After all that bait business? Do you know what happened? What kind of trouble I got into?"

Benjamin hung his head. "Sorry. Guests came in early for the big antique show downtown. Mom kept me working until dark, getting suitcases in, helping with dinner. Tried to get away once, but she caught me."

Missy's glare softened a little. He thought she was pretty. Maybe she'd forgive him. Still.

"I could've drowned Clarence. To say nothin' about me goin' down with him. Next time *you* get to be the bait."

"Deal."

"On second thought, nix that. Pa threatened me within an inch of my life if I do anything that stupid again."

Benjamin shot her a nervous grin when the bell rang and they walked into class. She'd about made it to her desk when Joe Bob Daniels, quarterback and cutest guy in school, turned and smiled.

She looked around to see if someone was behind her. Who was he smiling at?

Joe Bob stood up, motioned to the other kids, and started clapping. Everyone applauded. Even Miss Terrell wore a tiny grin.

Why were they laughing at her? What had she done now?

Allison, the head cheerleader, reached over and hugged her. "Way to go, Missy," she said. "Way to shut down that creep."

Chapter 7

Another kid leaned over his desk. "Yeah. We heard about what happened yesterday at the river."

Heard about the river? She and Clarence? Missy wanted to shrink into the walls, but the applause went on. Kids high-fived her and each other. She looked around for Clarence. He wasn't there.

"All right, class, that's enough," said Miss Terrell. "Take out your grammar books and turn to page eighty-three."

Missy sat down. Things sure changed in one day. No longer a loser, she'd become a rock star. At lunch, Allison, leader of the small pack, made a space at her table.

"Sit with us, Missy. We want to hear all about it."

Missy'd never been invited to their table, much less been the center of their attention. Benjamin walked by and she nodded, but there weren't any seats left. Besides, Allison had more questions to ask.

"What did he say when he was hanging upside down? Was his fat belly hanging out? We want to know everything."

Missy tried to smile, but it was harder than she'd expected. Seemed like she should at least be polite. Hadn't she done a good thing by shutting down a bully? Pa'd taught her to always take up for the weak.

She'd taken up for them, all right. She'd about

killed Clarence. But who'd told the whole school?

"Come over to my house after school. We're going to hang out."

Allison was inviting her over? Missy'd promised to meet Benjamin. He'd understand. Chances like this didn't come every day.

Clarence showed up at school later that week. He looked about the same. The old swagger didn't seem as certain, though. He tilted forward a bit as he walked and didn't make eye contact with anyone.

She watched him as he passed a line of lockers, away from the main hub of the classroom, and kept walking. A group of guys hid nearby, but Clarence couldn't see them. As he rounded the corner, a small army of feet extended in front of him.

He toppled over into a giant heap with an *umph* and struggled to rise as the same feet kicked him over and over. She saw him wince as a sharp-toed cowboy boot landed in the middle of his ribs. He tried to protect his lower back from a hit to his kidneys. But he didn't have enough hands to protect against blows that pummeled him from every direction.

Where were the teachers? Kids had gathered and were cheering the attackers on. This had been planned. The cheerleaders had even created a new cheer for the occasion.

"Get me some, get me some, get me some Godzilla. Go, go, get'm!"

Missy stepped in, panicked. "Hey! Stop it."

"What?" Joe Bob looked toward her, shock on his face.

"You're hurting him."

"Are you kidding?" he asked, then turned to deliver

another kick.

Something had to be done. Missy looked around the hallway, but no adult approached. Even though the crowd was loud and raucous, no one appeared. She looked in the nearest classroom. No teacher. It was right before lunch, but there had to be an adult somewhere. She ran to get Miss Terrell.

Miss Terrell was grading papers and looked up as Missy ran into the room.

"They're beating up Clarence. In the hallway by the gym."

Miss Terrell's face turned white. "Come with me. We'll get Mr. Wintroble. You don't have any business getting close to that mob."

Missy started to follow her to the counselor's office, but instead ran the other direction toward Clarence. By the time she got back, he was a crumpled heap on the floor. The guys turned to leave while the girls still whispered and giggled in a tight circle. They scattered as Miss Terrell rushed down the hall.

"Clarence, are you okay?" Missy asked. Stupid question. He didn't say anything. Missy reached out to pull him up. He jerked his arm away.

"Are you injured?" asked Miss Terrell. Another stupid question.

Clarence rose up in slow motion, as if every muscle strained in agony. His nose was bleeding and swollen. Missy wondered if it was broken.

"Come with me to the nurse's station," said Miss Terrell. "Then we'll call your father."

Clarence didn't say a word. He sat up and leaned against a locker. The metal door creaked as he shifted his weight, then he shook himself like a grizzly that had fought off a pack of wolves.

He stood, then pressed his back on the locker. His eyes were closed, and he breathed with heavy gulps. Missy wanted to help him, but it was too late for that.

After what felt like hours, he opened his eyes, turned, and limped down the hall. They watched in silence as he exited the front door of the school and struggled down the steps outside. Then he was gone.

"That was so wrong," Missy said.

"Did any of the teachers see the fight?" asked Miss Terrell.

"No. I couldn't find anyone. Guess they were already in the cafeteria for lunch. Besides, it wasn't a fight. It was an attack."

"He'll be fine, Missy. Probably hurt his pride."

"Hurt his pride? They beat him up."

"I'll call his father."

"No. Don't. Please. I'll go by and check on him after school."

"You?" Miss Terrell looked at her with a quizzical stare.

"Yes, ma'am. I'm the one who started all this."

Miss Terrell kept staring, but Missy didn't have time to explain why she needed to be the one to go. As soon as the last bell rang, she grabbed her bike and rode to Cloverdale Estates. To the house she remembered from the day she and Benjamin had collided with their bikes and ended up in a heap on the lawn.

After pedaling into the circle drive, she ditched the bike, ran up the large veranda, and knocked on an ornately carved oak door.

Mr. Lucas appeared at the door, polite and composed. Missy wondered why he was at home so early. Maybe he was taking care of Clarence. Her words came out in a jumbled rush. "Hello, sir. Is Clarence okay?"

Mr. Lucas looked at her as if he had no idea what she was talking about. "He's fine. Why do you ask?"

Missy didn't know what to say. She stumbled over a few words, then realized Mr. Lucas was clueless. Maybe Clarence didn't want him to know what happened.

"Never mind," she said. "Just thought I'd see how he was doing."

"You can talk to him, if you'd like." He called up the stairs. "Clarence. Missy Needham's here to see you."

Silence.

"Clarence, come downstairs." Mr. Lucas's tone never left a settled calm. Missy wondered if Clarence had ever been yelled at. Mr. Lucas barely raised his voice.

"He must've left. I'll tell him you came by." And in that moment, Missy was dismissed. She backed up, and the door closed with a firm, certain thud.

Missy turned to go. Looking back to a window upstairs, she saw a curtain move. Clarence stood, face swollen and bruised. Then the curtain fell.

Later that week, Clarence showed up at school again. He held his arm next to his chest and limped. The grimace on his face wasn't for show. He was still in pain. Every time he walked into a class, into the cafeteria, or anywhere in school, kids booed and hissed. *Loser*, *Godzilla*, *Gigantor* were some of the names. Most were worse.

She should've felt good. She'd taken out the

biggest bully in school. Single-handedly. Well, almost. Hadn't she done everyone a favor? So why did sadness fill her belly?

It was as if Clarence carried a scent, like blood to a shark. His injured self and the appearance of weakness invited abuse. Only this was the bully being bullied. Wasn't that different?

She was still getting invited to stuff. Benjamin had stopped coming around, but he was probably busy with his inventions. Someone was always grabbing her arm and saying, "Let's go." She went on shopping trips and was the subject of a makeover at Lindy Matthew's house. All the girls gathered around, oohing and ahhing. How her scarlet curls had somehow become a sensation was still a mystery.

Joe Bob smiled and winked when she walked down the halls as the new-and-improved model of Missy Needham. It felt good. Mostly.

Pa looked at her funny. He wasn't used to seeing her adorned with makeup, her hair tamed by Dippidy-Do. She even slept with orange juice cans wrapped around wet strands, resulting in a kind of hair she'd never seen before. Straight and shiny. Not much sleep, but it was worth it.

It was a new look for Pa to get used to. But that was okay. Besides, they'd had good news. Seemed that DNA test the sheriff's department was going to run on Pa's knife was really expensive, and the county didn't have money for it. Sheriff Davis was doing his own investigation. He'd clear Pa, no problem. All this mess with Pa's knife would take care of itself, like he'd said.

The next Tuesday was January 28, 1986. Funny that she remembered the day, except she'd been looking forward to it for weeks.

It was cold. The coldest day Missy could remember. She'd pulled every warm sweater she could find from a small stash of winter clothes at the top of her closet. Even then, the air sucked warmth out of her body as she raced to school.

Televisions were set all over the cafeteria. A teacher named Christa was going into space with six other astronauts. She'd made plans to teach from up in space. What a deal. Missy could think of several teachers she wouldn't mind seeing launched into outer space.

The cafeteria wasn't built to weather much cold. Large windows had webs of frost like connect-the-dot puzzles, and a frigid chill filtered in through the doors leading out to the playground.

The cool kids all sat at one table. Missy was in the middle of them. Benjamin sat in the back, by the door. Clarence was at the other side of the room. She tried to catch his attention, but he looked straight ahead.

Teachers called for quiet when TV screens showed bleachers filled with astronauts' families at Cape Canaveral. Steamy breath filtered around smiles and hugs. It was frigid in sunny Florida, too.

Missy wondered what it would be like to be launched by a capsule into an orbit that circled the earth. She was pretty sure Clarence would be glad to be anywhere but where he was right now.

The take-off looked good. A rushing geyser of fire and smoke fueled the rocket and shuttle upward. Up, up into the sky where all that could be seen of the rocket was a blast of smoke and fire.

Then, an explosion. Two tendrils of smoke

separated and launched into the atmosphere. Another fiery ball hurtled to the ocean below.

Maybe the shuttle was separating from the booster. Most of the kids didn't seem to think anything of it. They were barely paying attention, talking, taking advantage of a break from boring lectures. But the teachers gasped and covered their mouths.

Something was wrong. Missy watched the astronauts' families and friends leave their seats. There were hugs and tears. They rushed from the bleachers. Some left in couples, others in small groups. They dodged a reporter who hovered with a mic.

Coverage moved back to the announcer but the kids around her were too loud to hear what he was saying. He looked speechless for a moment that stretched too long for national T.V.

Most of the school still didn't know anything had happened. They were too busy flirting and carrying on like this was a holiday instead of a moment in history. Missy turned to Joe Bob.

"Is everything okay? That didn't look right."

"Whatever. It's fine. There's a big explosion when the shuttle separates from the rocket. Or something like that."

She didn't hear footsteps approach from behind, but she heard his voice. It was Benjamin.

"They're gone."

She turned to face him. "What do you mean?"

"Something went wrong."

Missy didn't want to believe him. For once, his genius mind missed the truth. Nothing like that could happen in front of a bunch of school kids.

"Joe Bob said it was normal."

70

Benjamin shook his head and walked away. She looked at Clarence and watched as his head bowed and chin crumpled. Tears ran like streams and dripped along his jawline, down his neck, and onto the collar of his T-shirt.

Powerful sadness flooded every wall built against it. She watched Clarence, invading a moment where she didn't belong but couldn't exit.

Chapter 8

That night, President Reagan appeared on national news to give the State of the Union speech. He spoke to students who'd gathered from classrooms all over the nation.

"I know it's hard to understand, but sometimes painful things like this happen," he said.

Missy thought about the day she'd tried to jump on the gurney that carried Mama out of their home. The day something died inside her.

President Reagan continued. "The future doesn't belong to the fainthearted. It belongs to the brave. The Challenger crew is pulling us into the future, and we'll continue to follow them."

Pulled into the future by disaster? Nothing about that made sense. She hoped it never did.

The sun shone again the next day with more record-breaking cold. Missy poked her head outside to check on Ranger. He ran in circles, chasing an imaginary squirrel, yelping and leaping as if it were a spring morning instead of the dead of winter.

She'd added bacon grease to his dog food and brought a couple more blankets to the shed. Ranger noticed her and barreled up the front porch carrying a mangled softball in his mouth. Time for catch.

"Hang on, boy. I'll be back." She added an extra sweatshirt over her T-shirt, then smashed a worn stocking cap over her curls. Pa looked up from sausage gravy simmering on the stove.

"You're going out? Only a quick game. And feed him extra again tonight. He needs more calories with all this cold. So do I." He held out his belly like Santa Claus and *ho, ho, hoed.*

Missy laughed as she went out the door, thankful that they were back to normal again. Pa didn't have much of a belly, even when he tried to stick it out. "Save some biscuits for me, Santa."

Her fingers were cold and achy by the time Ranger finally plopped on the front porch. He shifted his nose toward the county road as Sheriff Davis pulled off the road in his squad car. His deputy, Bill Hughes, was with him.

Strange. Why did he need the deputy? Pa stood inside the screen door as they walked up the porch steps.

"Hal. Have a warrant here for your arrest."

Missy's heart clenched. Not first thing in the morning. Not when they'd just been laughing at Ranger and about to polish off a hot breakfast.

"On what charge?" Pa's voice quivered.

"Murder, first degree." Emmett was grim and his words sparse, as if any extra words would somehow spiral this event into something even worse.

"Evidence?" Pa didn't have any extra words, either.

"DNA test results. The blood on your knife is Ephraim's."

Someone had paid for a DNA test? The county couldn't afford it. Someone else had to have come forward with the money. Only the real murderer would want Pa arrested.

Pa didn't move, didn't flinch, but his face paled. His hand shook.

"The warrant includes authority to enter your home, if necessary."

Pa stood, hand on the door, but didn't move to open it.

"Hal. I remind you that anything you say can be used against you in a court of law."

Still, Pa said nothing.

"Please." Emmett took a deep breath. "Don't make me open this door." In spite of the unnamed junk between them, Emmett's face was pained and his eyes dull.

Pa took a breath, pressed his fingers on the latch and opened it.

It was so quiet. Shouldn't someone be yelling, crying, carrying on? Like her? She stood in shock, couldn't move, much less protest.

Finally, she found her voice. "He wasn't there. Somebody put Ephraim's blood on that knife. Can't you understand? Pa's innocent. You—"

"Can't decide that here. Only doing my job," said the sheriff.

He put his hand on Pa's shoulder. Pa flinched, then walked with him out the door as the deputy followed. The sheriff turned to Missy. "Adele Phillips will be here soon. You'll be staying at the shelter. Court order."

"What? No. I'm staying here."

"Missy…" Pa tried to soothe her.

"What about Ranger? Who'll take care of him?"

"Maybe you can check on him after school." Pa glanced at Emmett, but he looked away.

"But he'll miss me...you. Who'll play catch with him?"

Sheriff Davis led Pa down the porch steps toward the squad car. He touched the top of Pa's head as he guided him into the backseat.

She ran after him and shouted, "You can't do this."

"Missy, it'll be okay," Pa said.

"No!"

"Adele will be by in a few minutes. Best get some clothes packed." Sheriff Davis situated his belly behind the steering wheel and started the car.

"I hate you. Hear me? I hate you...worthless tub of lard."

Pa pressed his hand against the back window. It was his sign. The hand he held up when he needed to be heard. When she was flying off the handle and he couldn't get a word in edgewise. When the tiniest gesture meant, *Don't worry. I've got this.*

No gravel spun as the squad car pulled away. Emmett Davis was careful with his precious cargo. Missy, on the other hand, hurled dirt and shouted insults.

"You fat mother...You stink like..." She raced after the squad car, sounding like a desperate two-year-old. Yelling, throwing things and hoping that any of it worked.

But none of it did. She fell to her knees, and Ranger loped over to lick her face. She held close, rocking him in her arms like a baby. Only she was the baby. Neither of them left that spot on the gravel until an old, brown Oldsmobile pulled off the county road and turned onto their lane.

The car had some kind of insignia, as if it needed

the weight of the law to carry out its job. Missy recognized Adele Phillips, the shelter's house mother. She nodded at Missy as she pulled the car alongside her and Ranger and rolled down the window.

Jeremiah Lucas and Ephraim had hired Adele to live at the shelter and take care of the girls. She looked like a combination of cop and drill sergeant. Nobody was going to cross her. She watched the woman climb out of the car and close the door with the authority of a general.

"Missy Needham," she said, her name a command, not a greeting.

Missy stood but kept her hand on Ranger. He growled.

"My name is Adele Phillips from the shelter. I'll meet you at the house. You can put your things in the trunk."

She hadn't thought about packing. What would she take?

"What about Ranger?"

"No dogs allowed at the shelter."

"But…" Missy tried to think of someone who'd take him. Joe Bob? Allison? She tried to imagine one of them taking care of her stinky mutt. No visions of tender loving care came to mind. "What will happen to him?"

"I can't address that. I'll meet you at the house."

It was a long trudge back to the house where Adele stood at the front porch. Walking up the steps without a word, Missy pulled Ranger into the house and closed the screen door. The woman walked in without an invitation.

Ranger crouched like a burglar by the front door,

whining and looking back and forth from her to Adele. He knew he was on illegal territory.

"Stay, Ranger," said Missy.

She turned on her way upstairs and watched, hoping that Ranger would remind Adele she wasn't welcome. Instead, he'd left his stance by the door and sat beside her, nuzzling her hand as she patted him. Traitor.

Missy looked under her bed, in her own closet, and finally found the old tweed suitcase in Pa's closet. After dragging it back to her room, she put it on the bed and sat down beside it.

She'd entered another space, launched like those astronauts into who knew what. Looking out the window, she considered slipping out without notice. Where would she go? Who'd break the law to take her in?

She pulled a sweater from the closet floor, noticed a hole in front, and tossed it back where she'd found it. Mama looked at her from her picture on the nightstand. Her dark curls blew in a breeze as she sat under the pecan tree out front. Pa'd found her sitting there and snapped the picture. She'd always been busy. And happy.

How had Missy and Pa ended up here? Things would've been different with Mama around. Missy wouldn't be trying to figure out what part of her life to pack in a suitcase, to show up in a place she'd never planned to go.

Sitting with Mama's sweater bunched up in her hands, she drew it to her face, then stuffed it in the suitcase. She turned to the window and saw a tiny chickadee perched on a lone branch. Missy guessed it was too cold for much singing. She was too sad to care, anyway.

It was almost time for school. How would she explain to the office secretary that she was late because her daddy'd been hauled off to jail, and she was sentenced to time at the shelter?

Shelves that lined her walls were filled with books and knickknacks from years of state fairs, whittlin' contests, and pictures too precious to store away. She spotted a tiny blue hippo she'd won at the fair when she was six and put it into the suitcase.

Along with the hippo, she tossed in cotton balls, an almost empty box of tissues, bag of Airheads, and a dog-eared copy of *Curious George*. She remembered her comb and the orange juice cans, then shampoo. But forgot to tighten the lid and watched it trickle in a stream at the bottom of the suitcase.

She got a towel, wiped it up, found a clean towel and put it in. Remembered jeans and put a pair in from the laundry pile. Then stuffed an economy size package of Sani-Hands under the socks with a flashlight. And at the end, she grabbed an old pocket knife that was nicked and worn with use. Probably didn't allow whittlin', but she'd have it in case she needed it. She drew in a long breath of air and blew it out. It was a pretty sorry weapon against an enemy who'd only laugh at a dinged pocket knife in her hands.

Missy looked back down the stairs. Adele held a clipboard and took notes, most likely documenting her exit. Ranger had settled himself at her feet, his chin resting near one clunky orthopedic shoe.

She went back to sit on the suitcase so it would close, then clipped the latch, and thumped it down the stairs. "Got one more thing to do," she mumbled in Adele's direction.

She dragged a half-empty bag of dog food from the shed and filled Ranger's dish. Pulling out the largest bowl she could find, she filled it with water from the green hose. At least it wasn't frozen. One more trip to the back porch and she found another old blanket for the shed. At least Ranger had a warm place at night.

Was the shelter like jail? Would she be able to visit him? There were too many unknowns to track in her brain. She filled the bowl with more dog food and a pan with more water until it sloshed over the sides.

"Hey, boy," she whispered to Ranger. Warm tears became icy on her cheeks, and she turned her head so Adele wouldn't notice. She led the dog outside to the tree where she'd positioned his food and water. Then sat down beside him.

"I'll be back, buddy. Don't you worry, now. We'll play catch and…" Missy tried to hold down the sobs, but they broke loose anyway. Ranger whimpered, wagged his tail, and licked her face.

How was she going to walk back to the house? With her heart at her feet, they felt too heavy to move. Adele came out the door with her suitcase.

"Have a key?"

In Avalon? When had they ever locked the door?

She found a key tucked in the back of the junk drawer in the kitchen, locked the door, and put it in her pocket. Adele already had her suitcase in the trunk and sat in the driver's seat, waiting.

She wanted to give Ranger one more hug. But another goodbye would kill that last little part inside that dared to believe Pa when he'd said it was going to be okay. She got into the back of the car and shut the door.

Adele didn't waste any time. The Oldsmobile roared to a start, hit a gulley in the driveway, and pulled out.

Ranger yipped and followed the car until he wore out and headed back home. As they weaved through familiar neighborhoods toward the shelter, Missy wondered how a town she'd known all her life had suddenly become a prison. Without a home, without Pa. And now without Ranger.

Chapter 9

The vehicle wound along a tree-lined boulevard to the end of a quiet street where a white-framed Victorian house with latticed windows and a wraparound porch rested in the landscaped yard. Even in winter, hedges were trimmed in neat corners and the remnant of flowers filled beds outside. A large sign engraved on a bronze plaque attached to the wrought iron front gate announced that they were entering *Katherine House*.

Pansies dangled from the sides of Grecian urns on each side of the front door, their happy faces wilted in the cold. Missy slipped on one step and caught herself on the railing. She paused at the door. What hid behind those doors that were supposed to protect her?

She'd seen some of the girls from the shelter at school but didn't really know them. What would it be like to live with a bunch of females? She only knew about Pa, who was stern, but usually the friendly sort— at least after coffee in the morning. Besides, he was family and that made home a comfort. Not much of that here, though.

Missy felt ages of the past as she walked inside the house. Maybe Yankee soldiers had commandeered it in the War, tromping through those marble tiles with muddy feet and stretching out on feather mattresses, dirty uniforms and all. She was an outsider, too.

There were pictures lining the walls of unnamed

hairy-faced men and ladies with pinched smiles whose corsets were obviously too tight. Musty air proved windows hadn't been opened since the cold set in.

They walked by an old-fashioned parlor, complete with upright piano and prim velvet-covered chairs. Heavy brocaded drapes over its windows allowed only a sliver of light where icy frost etched a lacy pattern. A walnut staircase wound above a dining room where a long table lined with camelback chairs was positioned in the middle.

Light beckoned as she and Adele walked into an open kitchen with white metal cabinets and laminate countertops, warped with time and use. A ceramic rooster stood on the top of one cabinet near a mop of artificial greenery. China plates in brass holders rested above cabinets on the other side of the room.

Missy saw a door at the back of the kitchen. Maybe it led to a basement, aka dungeon. But as they walked closer, she saw it was only a back porch, full of gardening stuff. A door leading outside was bolted shut, with windows along the wall facing outside.

After a quick tour of the kitchen, they walked down a hall to Adele's bedroom and office, complete with desk, typewriter, and its own bathroom. Another spacious bedroom had a large window that overlooked a row of lilac bushes outside the back porch. Maybe someone who helped her look out for the girls stayed there.

Her room was at the end of the hall upstairs, right across from a bathroom that looked like it'd been renovated with showers and extra toilets. Missy looked out the window and saw it overlooked the same view she'd seen from the back porch. Whoever had that extra room downstairs faced the same lilacs, still a long way from blooming.

The room was cool, even though a metal radiator forced out a little heat. A dresser stood between two twin beds. Missy dropped her suitcase on the floor and turned to face Adele.

"Gwen Scott is your roommate. Any questions?" she asked.

Missy shook her head, although questions ran through her head like stampeding ponies. If ponies stampeded, that is. Who was Gwen Scott? She couldn't place her face with anyone she recognized.

"You're free to go to school—should be there in time for lunch. The shelter bus comes to the south side of the school at 3:35 promptly. Be there, or you'll have to walk."

Missy wondered if there was a bus going anywhere but to the shelter. The thought of a long walk delaying her first night there sounded way better than showing up on time.

She looked outside her window. There were the lilac bushes, looking bleak right now. Maybe she'd be back home before they bloomed.

Missy pretended that everything was normal when she went to school that afternoon. Nobody knew Pa'd been arrested. Nobody knew she'd been sent to the Katherine House. And she wasn't about to tell anyone. After school, she sat in the back of the bus and turned her eyes when the intersection appeared that led to home. She hurried to her room when she arrived at the big Victorian and tried to do homework until Adele yelled from downstairs for dinner.

Adele introduced her to the girls. Each one barely

acknowledged her presence. They ducked around her, going back and forth from kitchen to dining room carrying bowls of food. A couple of girls, Beatrice and Michelle, set the table for dinner while Missy poured iced tea into tall tumblers by each plate.

Beatrice looked like an Irish princess with pale skin and blue eyes. She moved around the table with a graceful sway, ignoring Missy as if she were an unworthy peasant. Gwen Scott stood in the background, arms rigid and fists clenched, causing the flames inked on both arms to wave in angry heat. Missy tried to smile, but Gwen scowled back.

Hoping for some privacy, she went outside to sit on the porch after dishes and clean-up. The evening was cool, and a breeze shifted the porch swing left and right, as if it were confused about the right direction.

She took a seat on the porch swing and pumped her legs like she had when she was little. The swing squeaked in protest, then shifted into a graceful sway. She'd relaxed for a quiet moment when the screen door slammed.

"Oh, crap. She's out here," said one of the girls. Beatrice walked over and stood over her.

"Move."

Missy wanted to move. She really did. But she couldn't. She sat frozen.

"I said, move," repeated Beatrice.

Missy tried to break from that stare, but it glued her in place. A glint of a blade flashed in the dim light filtering from inside.

Still, Missy didn't move. Beatrice lunged toward her and Missy wrapped herself in a ball against the wooden swing. From the corner of one eye she saw another figure appear out of the darkness and face her attacker. It was Gwen.

"Picking on somebody who can't pick back?" Beatrice turned, the knife in hand, and faced Gwen.

"Go ahead. Try." Gwen's hand hovered over her pocket.

It was a showdown of female titans. Beatrice wavered for a moment. Missy found her legs and dashed out behind the two opponents into the safety of the house. She paused inside and looked through a window, half expecting to see the dust of a brawl rise over the porch with blood spewing.

But it was quiet. She slinked upstairs to her room, longing to hide under the bed like she did when she was little and a thunderstorm raged outside her window. That wouldn't help much around here. There was no lock on the ancient doorknob, which was okay since her unlikely protector aka roommate would be arriving at some point.

Missy crawled into bed, clothes and all. She hid her head under one arm and tried to imagine herself at home in her own bed, listening to night sounds outside her window. Those thoughts only made her want to run back as fast as she could manage to Ranger, to home.

Instead of this place where everyone despised her and nothing around her made sense. She was still awake at midnight, counting tiny clicks of a digital clock on the nightstand.

Gwen came in, sighed giant sighs, and belched as loud as she could. It wasn't long until her breathing became a gentle rhythmic wheeze. Missy peeked out to see the flames on her slender arms relax as the girl slept, scrunched into a ball like a scared child.

Missy got up to look outside the window into the quiet night. A full moon lit the side yard, where the border of lilac bushes looked like small trees.

A shadow emerged from one of the bushes. Missy shook herself to make sure she was awake. It looked like a guy dressed in a black hoodie and pants. He reached up to a window on the back of the house. Flinging himself over the window casing, he disappeared inside.

Missy let out a war whoop and ran out into the hallway. "Intruder alert! Intruder alert!"

Adele stumbled out of her room and ran upstairs, curlers askew and bathrobe in a crooked cinch.

"What's going on?"

"I saw someone. He lifted the window and looked like he came into a room downstairs."

"Where?"

"I don't know. It was at the back of the house."

"Beatrice's room, you mean?" Adele headed back down the stairs, house shoes pounding the worn wooden stairs, hand gripping the railing to keep her from sailing forward. Missy followed her, close behind.

Adele passed her bedroom and pounded on a door across from hers.

"Open up this door!"

Beatrice appeared at the door in a cartoon flannel T-shirt over boxer shorts. She rubbed her eyes in the light.

"What?"

Missy peeked around Beatrice into the dark room. The window was closed. Adele turned on the lights, searched the closet, under the bed. No one.

"You're waking me up for no reason in the middle

of the night?" asked Beatrice.

"I saw someone."

Adele turned her focus from the room and onto Missy. "You're sure?"

"Someone was outside, hiding in the lilac bushes. I saw him open this window and climb inside."

"Obviously, there's no one here." Beatrice glared at Missy, then turned her back to them both. Missy felt smoldering heat drill through her heart.

"Adele…" said Missy.

"Go back to your room." Adele looked at her with a strange mixture of sympathy and disdain. "If Emmett has questions, I'll come and get you."

Gwen came into the hallway and snorted with contempt. "Nice try."

"What?"

"Don't get enough excitement in your life? Have to make up some?"

"That's not true."

"Thanks for the midnight wake-up call," Gwen said. "For nothing."

Missy climbed the stairs and sat on the edge of her bed, trying not to breathe loud or ruffle the sheets. She'd been sure…

Flashing lights of a squad car approached the house. A few moments later, other lights bobbed around outside the bushes. Adele's voice carried up the stairs. She was talking to Emmett.

Missy tiptoed into the hallway to hear what they were saying.

"…one of the girl's windows," said Adele. "Said he was hiding in the lilac bushes."

"Find anyone?"

"No. Went to the bedroom, woke up Beatrice. The window was closed. She looked like she'd been asleep."

"You there, Missy?" Emmett called her from the living room, as if he had built-in radar for known criminals. She walked down the stairs and stood at the doorway of the living room.

"That how you saw it?" asked Emmett.

She didn't answer. He wasn't getting anything out of her except bare facts. Why couldn't this town afford a real sheriff? Not a cheap imitation of a side-winding snake who didn't know his head from his butt.

"Pretty dark outside. Maybe an owl swooping down or raccoon?" he asked, ignoring her silence.

"Not unless owls and raccoons wear hoodies," she said, glaring at the portly sheriff. His eyes looked baggier than usual. Hard to keep all those criminals in line in this town with a population of 642, mostly law-abiding citizens. Pa'd whoop her for being sassy, but he wasn't here at the moment. Thanks to Sheriff Davis.

He acted as if he didn't notice her attitude. Shifting his stance, he leaned against the nearest wall. "See anything else?"

"He was all in black."

"Okay, my men and I will keep searching the perimeter."

Adele led Emmett to the front door. She stopped and looked at Missy. Eye to eye, silent.

Missy felt a hard place quake inside. She missed Pa. And Ranger. And her bed. But she knew what she had was more than most of the girls dreamed about. What right did she have to whine?

"I've heard you've got an imagination," said

Adele. "Don't use it around here. These girls have been through enough. They don't need your drama."

Missy nodded. She crept back up the stairs and crawled into bed, holding her arms around her legs, longing for home.

Chapter 10

Missy's eyes opened in gray light the next morning. She looked for the window over her bed at home but found only bare wall. Gentle snorts coming from Gwen in the other bed reminded her she was at the shelter. Missy lifted the bedspread and tiptoed around as she pulled on her clothes. After stuffing a few things in her backpack, she crept out the door.

There was Ranger, sitting on the front porch, wagging his butt and looking thrilled that she'd finally appeared.

"How'd you find me, buddy? Got a radar in that nose?"

He was probably hungry. She hugged his neck, resting for a moment in his warmth and feeling a trickle of slobber run down her back.

"Dang, Ranger. I gotta go to school in this shirt."

Better than not having him around, though. She pulled a pack of cheese crackers out of her backpack and watched as the dog swallowed them in one gulp. He'd probably been waiting here most of the night. She'd share her lunch from the cafeteria, such as it was, until she could get home.

The town was just waking up as she meandered down cobblestoned streets of downtown with Ranger loping nearby. Della Young waved at them from the sidewalk outside the Elite Café. She'd be making buttermilk biscuits for customers who were mostly farmers with not much to do but who had a lot to talk about.

The air was crisp, and any leftover sleepiness was long gone by the time she saw the courthouse ahead. Light from a single window by the front entrance was the only beacon in sight. Missy'd heard the jail was on the lower level, although she'd never been there.

Neither had Pa, until now. She motioned to Ranger to stay, grabbed a breath, and walked in.

The room looked like any other decrepit office downtown. It most likely had a place in Southern history Missy knew nothing about. Cracks lined the water-stained ceiling like a giant spiderwebs. Paneling on the wall billowed up over seams, looking like the warped slates of an old dock.

The only thing that moved the décor into the twentieth century was a large chrome arch that stood in front of a rectangular table. Must be the scanner she'd heard about on the local news.

The scanner was like some kind of x-ray machine that scoped out hidden contraband. Like more than an extra peanut butter sandwich. A young deputy sat at the front desk drinking coffee and teetering back in his office chair. He looked up, startled, when Missy entered.

"Help you, miss?"

"I'm here to see my pa, Hal Needham."

"It's kinda early."

"He's an early riser."

"I see." He gave her a once-over, then nodded. "I'll check."

He returned after a few minutes and motioned for

Missy to unload her backpack on the table near the scanner. She paused. No telling what she'd accumulated the past few weeks. Even Pa didn't see the inside of her backpack. It was private territory.

She pulled out a mostly eaten bag of chips, several spiral notebooks, a headband, an English book, and a few catsup packets. An assortment of hall passes, meal tickets, and Kleenexes were followed by a slingshot, which fell out as she shook the pack over the table.

"Take off your shoes and walk through the scanner."

She hadn't changed her socks for a couple days. Might be a tad ripe for so early in the morning. Walking with careful steps through the arched machine, she held her arms out like a scared penguin.

Beep, beep, beep! She jumped to the other side in case the floor opened up to swallow her.

"Remove whatever's in your pocket, then re-enter the scanner."

Missy dropped her house key on the table and walked through again. No beeps this time. She waited for his nod, then put her shoes back on.

"Follow me."

Missy followed him along a corridor to a room the size of a classroom. Several tables were positioned around the room with orange plastic chairs leaning against them. The glare from fluorescent lights jarred her senses and made her wonder how anyone knew what time it was. One window promised a tiny peek to the outdoors, but shades concealed its view. For all she knew, it could've been five in the afternoon instead of seven in the morning.

The officer closed the door behind him. A few

minutes later, he opened the door and led Pa inside.

"Hey, squirt." He smiled and reached out for a hug. Missy fell into him so hard he almost toppled over. She kissed his cheek and felt the tickle of stubby whiskers.

Pa always shaved first thing in the morning.

What other everyday things had been stolen? She peered up into the face she'd seen almost every morning of her life. Worry lines formed against his forehead and the soldier-like stance of his shoulders drooped.

There was a word she'd heard before. *Stricken.* Not a word she'd ever looked up in a dictionary or used in an essay. She'd felt it, though. Stricken was when life had hurled its worst at you. You might still be standing, but only by an invisible line held from some unknown place inside. A line that got thinner by the minute.

What if that thread broke?

These people didn't know the real Pa. The one who'd done his best to live right all his life. Missy felt her heart retreat a few more miles inside. It was more than she could bear to see him like this.

He tried his chipper voice. "How are you, champ?"

"I miss you," she whispered.

"Miss you, too."

They settled into chairs around the table. The seat was cold on her behind. A chill sneaked up from the concrete floor and up green cinderblock walls. Did Pa have enough blankets? What about a pillow?

"Are they giving you enough to eat? Coffee?" More questions than Missy could ask came billowing out. He needed her. She needed him. Didn't the sheriff know that? Or care?

She had to find a way to get him out of there.

Somehow. "What about Jeremiah Lucas? Can he help us?"

"If I had the money. Bond was set at fifty thousand dollars."

Might as well have been fifty million.

"How are things at the shelter?" Pa asked.

"Okay." Well, except for everyone hating her and some guy trying to break in. Pa didn't need to know all that.

"You stay put," he said. "I'll handle this."

Missy leaned over and grabbed his hand, trying not to blubber. It was time for a decision. One that hadn't been concocted in her imagination in hopes she could avoid what needed to be faced.

What had Pa said? About gathering sticks for a bridge not hers to cross? The bridge stood before her, shouting, *Notice me. I'm not going away*. She'd go see Jeremiah Lucas. Maybe he'd help them. He was the bridge she'd take. And hope that taking it would carry them both across this muddy river.

"Better head to school," she said, giving him one more hug. She left the room without looking behind, knowing that if she saw him walk away, she'd lose it. Nodding goodbye to the young guard, she picked up her backpack and stuffed everything back inside. The cool air rushed to meet her outside as she whistled for Ranger and headed for Countrydale Estates.

Ten minutes later, Missy stood at the door of the Lucas home and rang the doorbell over and over, shouting, "Mr. Lucas. It's me, Missy Needham."

Mr. Lucas opened the door, looking like he was ready to appear in court. For a fleeting moment, Missy wondered if he ever slept. Maybe he stayed ready for the public, for life, at all times.

"Come in, Missy."

"We need help." Her words spilled out before he could close the door or be called away. "Pa's gotta get out of that jail. He didn't do anything wrong. It ain't right. But we don't have the money for bail."

Mr. Lucas paused, as if he was considering options. His voice was kind. "I'll see what I can do. But I need more information about that night. What did you see?"

It all came tumbling out. Finally, someone she could trust and who could help. He'd been educated to help people who were unjustly accused. He unraveled mysteries and stood up for the ones whose stories needed to be heard.

After all, he'd formed the shelter with Ephraim after he'd lost his own daughter. That took a special kind of heart. The kind that could actually clear Pa's name and prove his innocence. Her gratefulness spilled out in one happy jumble.

"I didn't know who to talk to. Didn't know who I could trust."

Mr. Lucas put his hand on her shoulder. "I can understand that. Start at the beginning and tell me everything."

"Okay, so first, I lied. Said I didn't get to the river till early in the morning, but I'd been there for a long time. I'd forgotten Pa's knife out by a tree. Figured I'd run down there, get it, and then run home. It was raining hard. But I didn't want to lose that knife." She was babbling but couldn't help it. The words kept pouring out as she pled her case.

"I see. Do you know what time that was? We need to have an idea if you can remember."

"I don't know, sir. It was the middle of the night. It was raining, but I figured I'd run down, get the knife and come back home."

"What stopped you from doing that?"

"I heard flood waters rushing. Then saw lights inside the old warehouse. When I looked inside there were people kicking and stabbing someone on the ground."

"How terrible to see, Missy." His tone was compassionate. "Can you tell me what else you saw?"

"They didn't stop. Not for a long time."

"No one noticed you?"

She might as well tell him. "I was sort of hiding. Crouched in the mud."

"That's understandable. How long do you think you were there?"

"I waited till everyone left. Wanted to run home, but I thought maybe...Maybe I could help whoever it was on the ground."

"Very brave of you."

Missy looked startled. Nothing about her actions that night had been courageous. Still, it was nice of Mr. Lucas to say.

"I wasn't brave, Mr. Lucas. Except I didn't want to leave that...person alone. Wouldn't be right."

Mr. Lucas wasn't firing his questions, one after the other, like Sheriff Davis had. Still she was pouring out any information he might need to help her and Pa.

"Did you get close enough to see that it was Ephraim?" he asked.

"No. I heard something and ran home. Pa was already up, looking for me. He called Emmett."

"Did you tell your dad what you saw?" His tone

kept moving her forward, even through the details she'd tried so hard to forget.

"No. I was scared. And I hadn't helped Ephraim." She stopped for a minute and decided not to tell him about the man who'd threatened her. "I was chicken. Then Sheriff Davis came over with Pa's knife. Had blood on it."

"I hate to hear that, Missy. Where are you staying while your dad's in jail?"

"I'm at the shelter."

"Ah, the shelter. That must be hard, being so close to home but having to live with strangers instead."

"It's okay. And really nice of you to help the girls."

Mr. Lucas shifted closer and spoke quietly. "I understand what it's like not to have a family to protect you. Also heard there was some excitement at the shelter last night."

"You did?"

"I represent the shelter and the girls in court if they need me to. Work pretty close with Sheriff Davis because of that. Do you feel safe there?"

"Pretty much, sir."

"By the way, has your dad heard about the results from the DNA test?"

Missy swallowed. "I don't know." How did Mr. Lucas know about the DNA test? Wasn't that confidential? She took a step back.

Mr. Lucas turned to a built-in desk in the breakfast nook and opened a drawer. He pulled out a pen and sticky note resting on top of a red binder and scribbled numbers. A picture stuck out on one side of the binder.

That was weird. It didn't look like a picture album. Or coupons. And the kitchen wouldn't be a place where

Mr. Lucas would keep legal paperwork.

Missy faced a closet door that was opened part way. Mr. Lucas'd probably been on his way out the door when he heard her pounding and caterwauling out front.

The brim of a hat stuck out over the top shelf. A broad-brimmed rain hat. Like one she'd seen on a man at the river.

She pivoted around as Mr. Lucas looked up and handed her the note. "This is my personal phone number as well as the office number. Feel free to call any time."

Mr. Lucas turned to the closet to see what had caught her attention. Missy felt the air around her become a vacuum, sucking out the oxygen. Her head began a slow spin and she tottered on the cool marble tile. Mr. Lucas put a hand on her arm and squeezed it lightly. "Easy there, girl."

Come here, girl. The memory of those words and the terror they brought came rushing back. It was his voice. The one that had frozen her in place on a stormy night at the river. Her knees almost buckled. She and Mr. Lucas stood now, facing each other in silence.

She heard the click of a wall clock in the kitchen and fought to stand. Somewhere she had to find the courage to walk away. A door opened upstairs and Missy turned to see Clarence trudging down the stairs. He didn't notice them until he'd walked into the kitchen. Then he stopped and stood without a word.

The phone rang, piercing the air with its clanging. Once, twice, again. Mr. Lucas kept his position in front of Missy and locked his gaze on hers. Then he spoke. "Get the phone, Clarence."

Clarence lifted the receiver and answered quietly. "Lucas residence." He handed the phone to his dad. "It's for you."

Mr. Lucas turned and strode toward the phone. Missy sucked in gasp of air and rushed to the door. She waved a jerky farewell on her way out.

Mr. Lucas looked up from the phone and smiled. "Always nice to see you, Missy. We'll be in touch."

She walked out the door as quickly as she could without breaking into a frenzied run. Ranger was digging in the neighbor's flower bed and didn't pay any attention to her sharp whistle. She forced her feet to move forward and pulled deep breath into her lungs.

She'd painted a bull's eye on her own back. Jeremiah Lucas had been at the river. He'd known it was her all along.

She'd told Ephraim's murderer everything.

Chapter 11

Allison waved her over the next day at school. "Hey, sleepover at my house Friday night. We might have visitors." She winked and cut her gaze to Joe Bob. He and his buddies would be making an appearance.

Missy smiled. "Cool. I'll be there." She wasn't sure how that would work with Adele, but she'd figure it out.

At lunchtime, Missy walked up to the cheerleader's table in the cafeteria and looked for a seat. Allison shifted her backpack over the only empty one. The girls looked up, then back at each other. Weird.

"Hey, can't wait for the sleepover," she said, smiling at Allison.

No welcoming smile answered on Allison's face. Without changing expression, she spoke, facing Missy's gaze.

"Forgot to tell you. Mom and Dad have to be out of town. Had to cancel."

"Oh, okay."

Missy stood with her tray. No one made a move to let her in. Each one who'd hugged her neck, invited her on a shopping trip, or just carried on with small talk between classes froze into stony silence.

She stood for a second longer, then turned and pretended to look for another table in the cafeteria. She didn't trust her face to hide the hurt. A hole to crawl into would've been nice. She'd have to settle for a seat in the same cafeteria and embrace the humiliation.

Gwen pulled out a chair across the table from her. Her flames twitched, prepared for battle, as usual.

"No room at the mall chicks' table?"

Missy tried to grin. That didn't work.

"You know why, right?"

Missy didn't say anything, only looked down at her cooked carrots and mystery meat.

"They found out."

"Found out what?" Missy's voice squeaked.

"You know. About your change of residence." Gwen smirked and pointed a slender finger toward the cheerleaders.

"You won't have a place at their table ever again. Not with your daddy in jail and you living at the shelter. Get used to it. You're a *shelter girl* now."

Missy remembered seeing Adele walk into the Christmas Eve service last year with a group of girls from the shelter. The girls had followed her like assorted goslings and had gotten the looks, for sure. Mr. Peabody'd about fallen off his pew checking out one of them.

Pushed out of their homes and a spectacle everywhere they went. Homeless in a town where homes had stood for generations. Homeless because the place that should've been safe wasn't.

Missy sneaked a glance at Gwen and saw hardness around her eyes. Her tensed body read *fight or flight*. It was when, not if, she'd blow up like an H-bomb. Not much question about who'd offered the information.

Missy didn't want to glance at the cheerleader's table or look like she cared. Benjamin sat a few tables away with the nerds. Clarence lumbered out on his way somewhere.

Missy rode alone in back of the shelter bus and closed her eyes as they approached the turn to her house. Adele had given her permission visit Ranger as long as she was back by supper. It didn't take long to jump on her bike and head toward home. The air was crisp and sunlight tender, perfect for a game of catch.

Clattering down the gravel driveway, she searched around the yard and saw the tether, his toys, and his water bowl gathered under the tree. Ranger wasn't there. Who'd want to take her mutt dog? And what had they done with him?

She whistled, expecting to see Ranger bound in from the backyard. But no racing toward her from the back of the house, no bowling her over with his happy greeting. Just stillness.

"Ranger! Come here, boy. It's me." She ran through the pasture, calling. "Ranger. Where are you?" Her voice traveled from shout to a panicked screech.

Ranger was a social sort. He visited the neighbors on a regular basis, begged for tasty treats and was always happy to make a new friend. Everybody in the neighborhood knew him. But it wasn't like him to go far from home. She rode to the Taylors, neighbors who lived closest to their property.

The kids were already home from school and playing freeze tag. Whoever was *it* had already tagged several kids who stood as if they were frozen in place. She went to one of them, hoping to get some news on Ranger before a new race began.

"Hey, Jimmy." Missy knew the kid. She'd babysat him and his little sister some. He was a toot, but she didn't have any options right now. "You seen Ranger?"

"Nope. He gone?"

"Can't find him at home."

"Suppose he ran off with the coyotes? Timmy's dog, Blue, chased after a coyote pack last winter. Never came back."

"No. He ain't one to chase coyotes. Too skittish."

"Maybe somebody hauled him off. Heard they were puttin' dog meat in Spam these days."

Missy scowled and punched his arm. "Thanks for nothing."

"Sure. Check with the Murphys. Course their dog'd make short work of Ranger."

Missy turned and rode toward the Murphys' house, who lived a half mile down a dirt road. A lumber truck hauling long trunks of skinny pine approached from behind and stirred up fine red dust that filtered grit in her mouth and clouded her eyes. She shook her fist at the driver.

Holding the sweatshirt over her nose and mouth, she picked up her pace after the truck had traveled far enough ahead to keep her from choking on its dust.

The Murphys weren't home. No sign of their vehicles around the yard except an old Ford pickup with flat tires and a hood that stood open. A weathered shed listed to one side beside their mobile home. Straggly trumpet vine curled over a wooden porch that had seen better days. At the deep rumble of a dog's growl—not her sweet Ranger but one of their mean mutts—she turned and rode back to the road.

She didn't stop searching and calling even on her way back to the shelter. The pedals on her bike pounded with the rhythm of her heart. Where could he be?

She'd find a way to come back tomorrow. Explain the situation to Adele. Hope she'd understand how important it was. She'd find paper and make a bunch of signs tonight. Somebody'd send him back home.

Adele had her head bowed over the desk when Missy knocked on the door of her office. The door was ajar. She was poring over a stack of papers, lifting one, then another, as if she searched for the key to a mystery. Wrinkles around her chin melded into her neck. Criss-crossed gullies creased her forehead and around her eyes.

She wasn't paid to care about missing dogs, especially with all the bigger stuff other girls had to handle. But Missy had to ask.

"Excuse me."

Adele looked up. Her eyes were red-rimmed, her hair tousled as if she'd been crying or hadn't had much sleep or both.

"Yes?"

It sucked to live with a professional caretaker instead of Pa. Adele was busy and convinced Missy was there only to bring minor league drama to a big-league world.

"I can't find my dog." Dang, she couldn't help it. Her eyes teared up.

"Did you check with the neighbors?"

"Yes, ma'am. No one's seen him. Could I go back to the house tomorrow?"

"Be home by supper, same as tonight."

"Thanks." Missy's eyes rested on a plaque that stood on her desk. It was the name of the shelter, *Katherine House*, in a smaller version. Adele followed her gaze.

Small talk might break through the wall she felt between her and Adele since the intruder situation. Wall, nothing—It'd been ice from the beginning. Maybe she'd get a little more compassion if she acted like she cared about the shelter. Like by asking what the name meant.

"Was Katherine someone who stayed here?" she asked.

Adele's eyes focused on Missy. She didn't crack a smile, didn't waste words on casual weather reports or polite niceties. Only the facts.

"She never stayed here. But the shelter was built for women like her who needed a safe place." She stopped and studied Missy's face, then went on. "Katherine was Ephraim's daughter."

Missy sucked in a breath and shook her head as if she knew better. Adele had to be wrong. No way...

"I know his daughter, Mary Beth. She's got kids. And..."

"Katherine was Ephraim's oldest. Mary Beth was your age when her big sister was murdered by her husband."

"Murdered?"

"Drunken rage. Took in after her with a knife, then passed out. Didn't know she was bleeding to death on the kitchen floor until he found her dead body the next morning. Ran for cover, but Sheriff Davis and his men found him hiding in the Tuckers' barn."

Ephraim hadn't talked about Katherine. How had she enjoyed Ephraim's company so long and never known the part that had shattered him to the core? Maybe he hadn't had words for it. She understood that.

No wonder Adele wasn't the tender-hearted type. She lived in the middle of a steady stream of broken dreams and destroyed lives. Most likely chiseled off any soft places.

That night, Missy felt Katherine's spirit and heard her cry settle in the walls, whisper through the girls' voices, and rest in Adele's sharp eye. Katherine had been betrayed. Somebody who should've loved her had destroyed her.

Missy hadn't meant to, but she'd done that to Pa. She'd left his knife, and Mr. Lucas had used it to set him up for Ephraim's murder.

Nothing she'd done had helped. Worse, all her efforts had morphed into a weapon. Wasn't that what Mr. Lucas said that night in the darkness? That she'd pay with the one she loved most?

No help in sight, especially since she hadn't recognized a real friend when he'd been right in front of her. Benjamin was the only one who'd cared that she'd seen a murder. Or that she was bullied. Or that she needed some good press and announced her take-down of Clarence Lucas.

What had Pa said about not building bridges she didn't have to cross? She'd built bridges all right. And burned them just as fast.

Mr. Jeremiah Lucas, the most powerful man in town, had paid for a DNA test and made sure it implicated Pa. He'd led a mob to murder his friend. And no one would believe her, a ditzy fourteen-year-old with bad hair and worse judgment.

Ranger, the one who'd loved her without any opinion to the contrary, was gone. She covered her head with the slick bedspread and rocked back and forth like a ship alone in stormy seas.

In the end, losers lost. And that's what she did best.

By the time Friday arrived, the last thing Missy wanted to face was a pep assembly in the school gym. It should've been called *Misery Rally*. Especially now that she felt anything but cheery and didn't have anyone to sit with. Maybe Gwen would show up. Who knew, though? Gwen did what she wanted to do when she wanted to do it.

The noise in the gym pounded her ears like hammers of different sizes, all drumming out another beat. Like in English when everyone talked at the same time but multiplied by ten.

Missy'd planned all day what she'd do after school. First, she'd check on Pa, then Ranger. She'd brought nails, tape and a small hammer, along with signs she'd written about Ranger in her backpack. Wouldn't take long to get them up around town.

She counted minutes until the last basketball player with knobby knees and braces shot a hoop and exited the gym. As if the rest of the school needed permission to leave from a bunch of dweebs with baggy shorts and sweaty armpits.

Missy glanced toward the entrance as she made her way down the bleachers. Several police officers had gathered. She looked around for trouble. Was there a fight?

Kids were cheering, talking. No dust flew, no blood sprayed from punched noses.

Two of the officers stayed by the door. Two came forward into the crowd.

Then, Missy saw flame-inked arms pulled behind Gwen's back and cuffed. She struggled and jerked her

body against the officer's grasp.
        "Heard she beat up Mr. Wintroble."

Chapter 12

A familiar voice spoke beside her. It was Allison, still in her cheerleader's uniform, with the faithful followers close behind. Missy looked at her perfect hair, her makeup, and her confident poise. All proof that Allison possessed every place her feet graced. Missy wondered what she'd ever liked about her.

"Beat him up?" she asked. "Like how? He weighs twice as much as she does."

"You know what they say about Gwen."

"No. I don't."

"Well, let me tell you…" Allison ducked her head near Missy's ear, ready to whisper.

"Stop." Missy held up her hand, then put it over Allison's mouth. "She's my friend."

Allison slapped her hand away. "Your friend?"

"That's right. Besides, what do you know about anyone other than yourself and your pea-squat world?"

Allison looked with wide eyes, then harrumphed as she turned and chattered to one of her groupies.

Missy returned her gaze to Gwen. She'd have to yell to get her attention in this crowd.

"Gwen!"

Gwen looked at Missy and scowled. She turned her head to where Mr. Wintroble leaned against the door frame with his arms folded. A large red blotch with a purple bump in the middle covered one side of his face.

What had happened? And how had Gwen ended up in the middle of it?

February wind bit Missy's hands and her heart raced as she rode to the county courthouse. Pumping the pedals of her bike harder, she tried to figure out what was going on with Gwen. Mr. Wintroble? He seemed pretty harmless. What did he do that was so bad she lost it and attacked him?

Missy leaned over the handlebars and tried to keep up with the police car. When that didn't work, she dodged into back roads to save time. She pulled up as the officers helped Gwen out of the back seat and up the stairs.

The jail and police station were both situated in the bowels of the ancient county courthouse in the middle of the square downtown. A bronze statue of a Confederate officer sat poised on a gallant steed at the center of a sprawling front lawn. Facts about his illustrious past were etched in a slab of granite under the statue. But the towering live oak overhead had witnessed more history than a Rebel officer'd ever made. Probably seen more than its share of injustice, too.

Gwen's head was down, her shoulders bowed forward. Missy wanted to yell, to get her attention. But no words came to mind. A young officer held the door as she and the other officer walked inside. Missy knew if she waited, she might lose Gwen in all the unknown things that happened when someone was hauled off to jail. She hadn't seen the process with Pa. She hadn't been allowed to be there. He'd been all alone.

She'd make sure Gwen wasn't. She ran through the front door and saw them walk toward the scanner.

"Gwen!" Her voice choked and tears rushed to her eyes.

Gwen turned and looked behind her, then looked away.

"I'm gonna be here. I ain't leaving," Missy called.

Gwen didn't look back. Missy felt a hand on her shoulder. It was Mack, the young officer she checked in with when she went to see Pa.

"She'll be okay." He nodded toward Gwen.

"Be okay? She's only sixteen. She probably had a good reason for…"

Missy stopped. She'd never figured out what made Gwen blow without any warning. Why had she attacked Mr. Wintroble? Not that Missy disagreed with her choice of victim. Still, there had to be a reason.

Mack looked at her as if he cared. He'd let her in at the crack of dawn to see Pa, even though the time for visitors had been hours away. Kind, in spite of the hard stuff the law required him to watch over, day in and day out.

Mack opened an interior door to a young woman dressed in baggy scrubs who pulled a bucket of soapy water behind her. She started in one corner of the room and mopped with long, even strokes, looking up only once for a glimpse outside.

He turned back in her direction. "Want to see your dad, Missy?"

"No, sir. I need to see Gwen."

"The girl they just brought in?"

"Yes."

"Are you a family member?"

"No, but I'm her friend." Missy wasn't actually sure about that. Still, Gwen'd stepped in for her once.

She'd return the favor if she could.

"Right." Mack cleared his throat. "Heard she's from the shelter. The only person who can see her is Adele Phillips. Besides, you can't visit her unless you've got an adult with you."

Where was she going to find a good adult? Or at least one willing to take her along? Missy bolted out the door, got on her bike, and rode to the shelter. She blew in the front door, chest heaving and lungs panting. Adele was in the kitchen, unloading groceries. She jumped when Missy slammed the back door.

"What?"

"They've arrested Gwen."

"Why?"

"Don't know. Right at the end of the pep assembly. Something about the counselor, Mr. Wintroble."

Adele put a carton of milk in the refrigerator, grabbed her car keys, and headed out the door.

Ranger would have to wait. He had plenty of food and water. Hopefully he'd found his way home by then. Anyway, Gwen needed her more. "Can I come?" she asked Adele.

"If you promise to be quiet."

The brown Oldsmobile started with an intimidating roar. No conversation on the short ride to the station, Adele stared ahead and clenched her hands around the steering wheel.

When they walked into the front office of the police station, it was all *Yes, ma'am, No ma'am.* Within minutes they were talking to one of the officers who'd arrested Gwen.

"What are the charges, Dwight?"

"Assault of a public servant." The guard's face was

grim. He looked like he knew what all this meant and that it wasn't good.

"Assault?" Probably Adele knew, too. This was only looking worse.

"Can't tell you anything else right now. Charges are still pending."

"Can I see her yet?"

"Give us a few minutes. Have to get her processed. Do you have an attorney for the shelter?"

"Of course. Jeremiah Lucas."

"Okay. She needs representation. It looks bad for this young lady."

Missy twirled one strand of hair over and over. Her stomach growled with hunger, and she was thirsty. Bright afternoon sun had turned to dusk by the time Gwen walked into the visitor's room.

"What happened?" Adele reached over and tried to take Gwen's hands into hers. Gwen tugged away and sat like a stone, staring ahead.

"You have to tell me," Adele said. "I want to help."

"Right. *Help*." Gwen's words came out like pistol shots, sharp and angry.

She wasn't the only one who could get mad. Adele rose out of her chair and faced Gwen with a steely jaw and hands planted on her hips. "Stop this nonsense. Tell me what happened. Now."

"Mr. Wintroble." Gwen snarled the name, then spit as if it tasted like lye soap.

"What about him?"

"He called me into his office. Said he'd heard about a modeling job available in the city. Asked if I was interested. I was like, are you kidding? Me?

"He told me I didn't know how beautiful I was.

Gave me the creeps, but I thought maybe…Said he needed pictures, that he'd send them on to the agency. Invited me over to his house—had a studio set up in the back."

Gwen's face lost some of its color as she continued. "I stood up and said, 'No way.' "

" 'You don't want the job?' he asked. 'That agency will take you out of the shelter, bring you to the big city where you'll make more money than you ever dreamed.'

"I turned to leave, but he stood by the door.

"I decked him. So hard he fell on the floor. Then ran out. He must've called Sheriff Davis before I could tell him my side."

Adele's face was now as white as Gwen's. "You've got to tell him what happened."

"Who will believe me? No witnesses. I have a reputation."

"We'll help."

Missy nodded. But she knew they'd have to call upon some mighty special help. It was the worst possible scenario, an adult's word against a shelter girl. No witnesses, no proof that the counselor had done anything to make her lash out.

Gwen's eyes flooded. Missy wouldn't have believed the girl ever cried. Stupid to think she didn't. There was probably an ocean of tears under all that ink. Missy watched Adele for a clue, any signal of what to do or say.

"Look at me," said Adele. Tiny hope ran like a lifeline from Adele's eyes to hers. "I'll get to the bottom of this."

Gwen sniffed, then nodded, not breaking their

gaze.

Adele might not be big on sweetness, but she could be trusted. Gwen knew that.

As they left, Missy turned to Adele. "I need to see Pa. Is that all right?"

"Be back by dark." Missy watched her march out the door. Her backside shifted and shoulders leaned forward as she angled into the driver's seat of her car. She pulled out, but instead of turning in the direction of the shelter, drove toward the school. She'd find answers, and God help anyone who got in the way.

Missy turned and walked to Mack's desk. She'd already taken off her shoes and was ready to go back through the scanner. He smiled and she nodded back, unsure of what to say. It was getting late, but she needed to see Pa. Maybe he'd understand.

"I think you're okay," he said. "Visiting hours are about over, though. Can you make it quick?"

"Sure." She put her shoes back on and peered around for Pa in the visitor's lounge. A couple sat together at one table, heads pressed close to each other and hands clasped as they talked. A little girl dangled her legs from her daddy's lap and played with his denim collar on the other side of the room.

Pa came in from around the corner. He sat down and held out an arm for Missy to nestle into.

"Hey, Pa," said Missy.

"Doin' okay?"

"I miss you. Lots. Heard anything from Mr. Lucas?"

"Not yet."

"Umm." What to say? She didn't want to scare Pa but needed him to tell her what he knew about Mr.

Lucas. "How well do you know Mr. Lucas?" she asked, sitting as close to him as she could.

"Knew him when he was younger," he said. "Why?"

Missy shrugged her shoulders. "Just wondered."

"Don't know why you need ancient history, but we were in high school together. Along with Emmett Davis and Adele."

"You knew all three since high school? I thought Mr. Lucas was from Birmingham."

"He finished his law degree and had a practice there for a few years. But he was born and raised in Avalon. His mama died when he was fifteen, and he went to live with Ephraim and his parents."

"Ephraim? He lived with a black family? Wasn't that weird back then?"

"It went cross-wise against the culture, for sure, but Jeremiah's family wasn't exactly high society. They lived across the river in a tiny shack. Long before the projects were available to poor families."

"Mr. Lucas was from a poor family?"

"Raised by his granddaddy and mama. Don't know where his daddy was, just that things were hard. Granddaddy drank away most of the money his mama brought in doing laundry and cleaning houses.

"Ephraim's parents lived nearby. Nice people." Pa paused and looked out the window.

A breeze shifted the branches of a spindly tree outside and Missy watched his gaze move toward the window. Could he hear the birds sing in the early morning? What was it like not to be able to fire up his pick-up and drive off to work every morning?

Did he miss breakfast together as much as she did?

Or stabbing soft earth with his shovel, getting the garden ready for spring? Maybe looking outside helped. Unless it reminded him how life went on without him.

Pa looked back at the table and then to Missy. "I remember how he ate like he hadn't seen food before. And the day when a bird swooped down and smacked Jeremiah in the head. He went into crazy mad. Got a pellet gun and shot that bird. Over and over, even after it was dead."

Mack was stretching the time limit, acting like he didn't know visiting hours had been over for ten minutes.

"Everything changed when his uncle showed up. Jeremiah couldn't hang out with us anymore. Went to law school after college and had a practice in Birmingham for a few years."

"Why did he come back to Avalon?"

"Said he just wanted to get back home. Got tired of city life."

"What happened to his mama?"

"Don't know for sure. Why?"

Missy shrugged. There was too much to say and not the right time to say it.

"How can we get you help?" she asked.

"Mr. Lucas would be a good attorney. But I don't have the money to hire him."

A good attorney? A good enemy, Missy thought. One who'd use any information Pa gave him against them both.

"Maybe we could find another one. There's got to be a way," she said.

"There's always a way." He patted her shoulder and tried to smile. Still taking care of her no matter what. Why couldn't she return the favor and help him when he needed it?

Missy rested for a minute beside him. She wanted to tell him about the cheerleaders. And Ranger. And what she was pretty certain she knew about Jeremiah Lucas. And he knew about her.

But Pa didn't need any of that right now.

Chapter 13

Back at the shelter, Missy tracked Adele down. She'd tell Adele about Mr. Lucas and see if she could help. She was an honest woman, and strong. But how would she feel about hearing one of their founders had probably murdered the other one?

Adele was in Missy's room, changing the sheets on Gwen's bed. She stood up when Missy came through the door. Something about her body looked like a giant sigh. Missy's insides choked up. She couldn't accuse an adult like Jeremiah Lucas with what she suspected, not unless she could prove it. Adele didn't operate in *think so's* and *maybe's*.

Instead, she'd face the matter at hand.

"What are we going to do about Gwen?" Missy asked, hoping that Adele heard the "we" part.

"Don't know. Plan to figure it out, though."

"Pa said he went to school with you. And Emmett and Mr. Lucas."

"That's right." She plopped down on the bed, as if tiredness had zapped her last bit of strength. Missy paused, then sat beside her. Not too close, but in the same vicinity.

She needed to know about those years when she, Pa, Emmett, and Mr. Lucas had been young. Maybe there were some clues there. She took a breath, hoping her question wouldn't sound like an interrogation. And that Adele wouldn't get spooked.

"Were you and Pa friends with Sheriff Davis and Mr. Lucas?" asked Missy in a soft voice as Adele closed her eyes. She was quiet so long, Missy thought she'd forgotten she was there.

Finally, she spoke. "Until the night we graduated from high school."

Missy ventured one more question. "What happened?"

Adele looked at her, then at the floor. She clasped her hands in front of her, as if she wasn't sure what to do with them. "There was a drowning at the river. A friend of mine."

Missy tried not to gasp. She thought about Clarence and how he'd almost drowned. And would have, if Pa hadn't shown up. "Who was it?"

"Her name was Janie Truett. We were neighbors when we were little. Spent lots of hours exploring, hanging out together. Grew into teenagers, fell in love every other week, stayed friends through it all.

"Don't know what happened." Adele stopped again. The hallway was quiet, the shelter still, as if they waited, like Missy, for her to go on.

"The party was on the beach near our favorite cove. Maybe she'd been showing off. Don't know how she could've slipped in without notice. She'd died alone right in the middle of a bunch of people. We were the bunch of people.

"Still haunts me. Can't figure out why I wasn't there when she needed me."

Missy felt as if she'd been tossed into a painful secret with kids in another time. Ones who'd seen what kids should never have seen. Like her, they'd stored it inside, only to find it pop up in the quiet, unwilling to be forgotten.

Missy had to ask a question that she knew was somehow rooted in history she hadn't been a part of.

"Did Pa and Emmett hate each other back then, too?" she asked.

"Hate's a strong word. Still, can't say they've had a fondness for each other since that night."

"Why?"

"The law had to rule out murder. That meant we were all questioned. Your daddy and Emmett got into a fist fight at the station. Lots of accusations flew around. Probably lots of regret. Both of them liked her."

"Pa liked Janie?"

"That was years before your mama. He was just a kid."

"Did they ever figure out why she was swimming in the river at night?"

"No. Sheriff's department closed the case and called it an accidental drowning. That didn't mean it was closed with us kids."

It was hard to imagine a young Adele. She'd had a friend who'd died, too. And no one knew why or how. Missy's mind flashed back to Ephraim's body, shaking with blows. And the silence when he could no longer cry or struggle. When his life slipped away on a rain-soaked night of terror.

Could she tell Adele? Would she care? Probably. But today it was time for Adele's story.

Adele lifted her shoulders and stretched one hand over to rub her lower back, as if she was in pain. Still, she kept talking.

"Always the unanswered question, *Why didn't I*

notice she was gone until it was too late?"

Adele stopped. She was done, but Missy had to ask again.

"How come Pa didn't tell me?"

"It was a long time ago. Probably figured it was better to move on with life. He met your mama a few years after that. Mr. Lucas left for college. Life kept moving on. So did we."

Adele stood up and almost smiled when she met Missy's eyes. "I'm sure it was more tangled than that. But that's all I can say right now."

"Oh. Thanks."

"Look. Life gets complicated. Don't make assumptions. Like with Gwen. Rumors will be swirling around." The friendliness in her gaze disappeared, and back was the no-nonsense woman Missy'd come to know. "Don't talk about anything you've heard about Gwen. Nothing. Could ruin a court case. Hear me?"

Adele stood, straightened her shoulders, and walked out the door. She turned for a moment and looked at her with…

If Missy didn't know better, she'd guess it was fear.

****

It was Saturday and Missy had a plan. Find Ranger. She saw signs she'd nailed to trees, and duct-taped to streetlights on her way to school every day. They were getting dog-eared and water-soaked, but still no responses from anyone.

After permission from Adele, she headed on her bike through town on her way home, looking this way and that, alert to an unfamiliar car or shadow lurking in alleys of neighborhoods she'd known all her life.

122

A scent of damp pine filled the early morning air. Dogwood blossoms sprinkled the woods outside of town, still bare enough to show off their beauty. On a rise above the river, she watched a fisherman guide his flat-bottom boat. It was crappie season. Before long, he'd be peeling off his coat and heading back home for a fish fry.

The house looked none the worse for their time away. A scraggly forsythia bloomed against the picture window. Pa would notice weeds already sprouting in his garden. And window trim that needed a fresh coat of paint. All she cared about was Ranger and he was nowhere in sight.

Missy parked her bike against the house and searched the perimeter of the house, hoping he'd hurtle around from the backyard, leaping like a happy kid.

Everything was arranged in perfect order inside the shed. Chew toys, along with the mangled soft ball, were placed in rows along one wall of the shed. His water bowl was clean and dry. The sack of dog food was folded into even pleats.

Not something she'd ever do. Or Pa. A chill overwhelmed her as she peered around the property. There was a trespasser who'd been checking out their home. Maybe watching her right now. And using Ranger to get to her.

Missy shuddered. She didn't want to think about Ranger alone and afraid against anyone who thought he might actually be a threat. Someone who didn't know he'd only run or lick them into submission. Did he have time to run?

She searched the ground for blood, for any evidence of a struggle. But everything looked normal.

Only way more perfect that either she or Pa ever kept it. What kind of intruder left things neater than they had been before?

Then she remembered seeing the inside of a locker at school. Extra shelves had been set up inside. Folders and books were stacked and organized in order of size and subject. Only one person had a locker like that.

Missy got on her bike and headed for the Inn. She turned into the tree-lined lane and saw a lean-to near the garage. It opened to the south, sheltered from the wind. Fresh hay cushioned the floor.

Ranger bounded out from behind a tree. She was about to yell at him when Benjamin appeared from the front yard and hurled a ball in the dog's direction. He leaped to snatch it, then ran back, tail flapping and butt wiggling to Benjamin with his spit-drenched prize.

She threw her bike to the ground and stomped up beside Benjamin.

"Stealing my dog? I've been looking all over for him."

"Steal him? Are you kidding?" Benjamin held his ground but looked confused as Ranger tackled her and licked her face. It was hard to stay mad lying on the ground with a bunch of dog slobber dripping down her chin. Her dog's slobber.

"I didn't know you could leave the shelter to check on him," he said, trying to explain before she decked him. "He was lonely." Benjamin scratched Ranger behind the ear. "Kept him fed, played catch. Only trying to help."

The relief of finding Ranger and knowing he'd been in Benjamin's hands all along bowled her over. It was kindness so over the top, she didn't have words.

Reaching up, she hugged him, swift and hard. By the time she released his neck, he stood speechless with a goofy grin.

She blurted out what she'd wanted to say since that afternoon in the cafeteria when the ones who'd appeared to be friends weren't.

"I've been a butt."

"What?"

"It's a long story. You don't have to forgive me. I understand."

Benjamin sat back on the ground. Ranger plopped his head into his lap. Missy sat down beside them.

"Could you take care of Ranger awhile longer? Might need some time to figure out this mess with Pa."

Benjamin took one arm and hurled it around her shoulders. She sat too far away for all this to work right. Instead of a proper side hug, his hand dangled in the middle of her back like a broken chicken leg. Missy scooted closer until they sat side by side.

He sighed with the sweetest awkwardness. A dimple creased one cheek, and dark lashes feathered over almost black eyes as he gazed down at her. Girls would pay good money for those lashes.

"Got a plan?" he asked.

"Plan?"

"You, Missy Needham, always have a plan."

"My plans only make things worse."

"It's not over yet."

"How do you know?"

He smiled, looking so proud he knew something she didn't. "We'll figure something out."

We. She liked the sound of that.

"I didn't think they'd let you leave the shelter,

except for school and stuff." He stretched his legs out on the damp grass.

"Well, it's bad, but it's not jail. Adele lets me check in with Pa every day. When I couldn't find Ranger, she gave me permission to look for him."

"How's your dad?"

"He won't complain. Kills me to see him in there and know it's my fault." Her voice caught midway, and a sob came up through her belly. Benjamin put his head over hers, and she cried into his soft collar. "I left his knife out there. Somebody got ahold of it and put Ephraim's blood on the blade."

"You didn't mean to leave the knife. It was an accident."

"There's something worse."

"What?"

His brown eyes squinted as he peered into hers. Benjamin cared. He'd extended a gift, his friendship.

This time she'd take it.

"I went over to see if Mr. Lucas would defend Pa," she began. "I had to ask, to find help somewhere. He wanted to know what I saw. I told him everything. Except about the guy who saw me. The one who was wearing this hat."

"Hat?"

"Like one I've seen in a Cabela catalog. I remember the rain dripping down off its brim at the river that night."

"What about it?"

"There was one like it in the closet when I was talking to Mr. Lucas. At least it looked like the same one. He saw me looking at it."

"Did he say anything?"

"No, but…I don't know what would've happened. Clarence came down the stairs, getting ready for school. I left—went back to the shelter. If he's the one who was leading that mob and he knows I know…"

"We've got to protect you."

"Like how? Mr. Lucas has money, everyone in town thinks he walks on water. People will think I'm crazy or just trying to get my dad out of jail. Besides, maybe there are other hats like that. But the way he looked at me when he knew I'd seen it… And he asked me about the DNA test results."

"Somebody paid for DNA testing?"

"A lot of money. The county sheriff's department sure didn't have it. Mr. Lucas asked me if Pa'd found out about the test results. No one knew about that. Only Sheriff Davis and his deputy. And Pa and me. Emmett wouldn't advertise that. It's confidential. If he told anyone, it might blow the case against Pa."

"Pretty good chance that Mr. Lucas isn't the man people think he is," Benjamin said. "That would make sense, knowing his son."

"Right. I get the feeling Clarence's been beaten up before. It's weird. His dad didn't even know he'd been attacked at school. He couldn't have missed his face and the way he limped. But he acted like he knew nothing about it."

"The plot thickens."

"Right. And now Gwen is in jail."

"Flaming arms Gwen?" Benjamin asked.

"One and the same."

"What'd she do?"

"Assaulted Mr. Wintroble. Said he came on to her, wanted to take pictures. Creepy stuff. She decked him.

"Where were you? Everybody in school knew by the time the cops hauled her out of the pep assembly."

"Dentist appointment. Left right after math, before the assembly."

Benjamin sat back against the trunk of the tree. He squiggled his brow and didn't say anything for so long Missy wondered if he'd checked out of the conversation to cogitate a new invention. When he finally spoke, it was with a question.

"Wonder if Mr. Wintroble is connected to Jeremiah Lucas?"

Well, that was out of the blue. How in the world did his mind work? Just when she thought his head was in a different universe.

"What makes you think that?"

"Mr. Lucas is the head of the shelter, right?"

"Right. But he founded it with Ephraim. They'd been friends for years. Can't imagine…Then again it sort of makes sense."

Benjamin leaned toward her with his hands stretched out toward her. "I'll help. Whatever you need, I'm here." Then he paused. "If that's okay."

Lord, what kind of goodness had she run into out of nowhere in Benjamin? And when had he gotten so cute?

Benjamin drew closer and Missy didn't back up. She closed her eyes, then squinted them open long enough to see his lips aim for hers. She popped her head up and smacked his nose on his way down.

They fell back laughing. Felt like a honey pot drifted over Missy's head and settled. But she had to focus on Benjamin's words. What had he said? Jumping up with flaming cheeks and heart pounding, she answered. "I…I do. I need help."

Benjamin laughed and said, "Okay, then. Let's start with the obvious. We'll call Sheriff Davis."

"What?" Missy looked at him, outraged. What was he thinking? "No. He's the one who arrested Pa. He's either corrupt or stupid."

"Finding blood on your dad's knife looked bad."

"Sure. But he knows Pa better than that. I don't trust him."

"What about Adele or Miss Terrell?"

"I don't know. Adele may still think I'm a drama queen. Miss Terrell seems kind of delicate for any real kind of help."

"Delicate is okay, if she knows what's going on. She has a good eye at school, sees a lot of the kids. Might be a possibility."

"Really? Only if poetry was a weapon. Of course, that's not to say she couldn't use it as one," said Missy.

"You *are* dramatic."

They brainstormed ideas until morning turned into afternoon but didn't come up with much. Being with Benjamin was like a refuge. The first one she'd found since Pa'd been arrested. She didn't want the afternoon to end. Still, she had to see Gwen. She'd promised.

"Gotta go see Gwen," Missy said. "Hoping Adele will come with me.

"Let me know how it goes." He smiled and turned toward her. She wished he'd kiss her again. On second thought, now wasn't the time to get distracted. She pecked him on the check, ruffled Ranger's neck, and ran to her bike before she could think any more about kissing Benjamin Eckstein.

Chapter 14

Adele stood outside the shelter, digging around the trunk of a large azalea bush. She appeared ready for spring in her overalls, orange plastic clogs, and bright pink floral gloves.

She looked up at Missy, distracted, but seemed thrilled to be outside digging in the dirt around an azalea bush. "Phytophthora's trying to overtake the root system."

Phytophthora? Root system?

Adele continued. "See how the leaves look wilted, even though we've had plenty of rain? Drastic measures must be taken to save it."

"Oh." It was a horticultural calamity, not an influenza outbreak. Good to know. Missy tried to look interested. She waited a moment and then spoke in her most polite voice.

"Could we...I mean, do you have time to see Gwen today?"

"*We* is a mighty big word for two letters. Finish your chores?

"Yes, ma'am. I mean, I will."

"Meet me at the jail around two. I've got some errands to run, then I'll stop by to check on Gwen."

Adele was at the jail and checking in with Mack promptly at two. Mack led them both into the visitor's lounge. It was hard to know Pa was so close, but she'd visit him after they'd seen Gwen.

Another lady sat at one of the round tables. Her back was to Missy, but whoever it was looked as if she'd just left the salon. Silky blond hair formed loose waves around her neck. As she pulled a strand behind one ear, a tiny silver hoop appeared.

It was Miss Terrell.

Adele spoke first as they sat down beside the teacher. "Rachel. How are you?"

"I'm fine. Worried about Gwen, though." Miss Terrell worried about Gwen? Missy didn't know Gwen had even hit her radar.

"Me, too," said Adele. "Did you talk to Emmett about what Gwen told us?"

"Sure. Although I wasn't there and can't prove anything except for what I know in my heart— Wintroble can't be trusted."

"Any evidence against him?"

"No. But young girls go to him looking for advice, for career help. Sometimes they're vulnerable. That's never good. Especially if the public servant is really a predator."

"Public servant?" Rage rose in Missy like bubbles from a boiling pot. "He's no servant in that school. Can't even find him most of the time."

Miss Terrell spoke as if she were teaching a class of eighth graders. "A schoolteacher, counselor—all are considered public servants. Can't say that punching Mr. Wintroble was a good idea, but I understand how it happened."

Missy thought about it. "Keep wondering why Mr. Wintroble didn't come around when Clarence was getting beat up. Seems like it would've been his job to at least be there. Not that he'd do anything."

"True. Mr. Durham was out of town that day. Mr. Wintroble should've been there to fill in."

It wasn't like their principal to step down in his duties, even for a day. Having Mr. Wintroble in charge gave her the willies.

"Bet you wonder how I know Gwen," said Miss Terrell.

"Did you have her in class?"

"No, never did. Of course, I'd spotted her in the halls."

"Spotted her?"

"I've got some history of my own."

Missy turned her chair to see a Miss Terrell she'd never seen before. What kind of history could a Southern belle have? That was worth talking about, anyway.

"I grew up with lots of craziness." Miss Terrell took a breath. "Mama made good money…Let's just say I was part of a profitable business. One day a kind teacher talked to me, took me under her wing. Even helped me get my teaching degree at Auburn. I made it my goal after I graduated to keep an eye out for hurting kids."

Mack let Gwen in the door. They looked up at her. Gwen walked up to Miss Terrell and gave her a hug. Missy stared in surprise.

"Rachel's been my friend for a while," said Gwen, as if in answer to Missy's question. "She noticed when I'd been out of school for a while. Took me to her house, cleaned me up, and got a restraining order to protect me. Nobody from home could bother me without getting arrested."

Missy sat, silent. She wondered what else she'd missed when she'd been wrapped up making her own world safe.

After school the next afternoon, Missy headed back to the shelter with another plan. Visit Pa as soon as she checked in with Adele. Maybe Mack would let her see Gwen, too.

She clambered up the steps of the shelter's ancient veranda and pulled on the screen door. It creaked and then slammed shut behind her as she peered into the sprawling family room. A wall clock ticked like a metronome in the stillness. She'd ridden her bike and beaten most of the girls back from school.

The door of Adele's office was partly opened. Missy could hear papers rustling and faint country music of the radio station she kept on while she worked. Missy tapped the door quietly, hoping she wasn't interrupting some unknown project to save the world.

Adele barely looked up from the papers that cluttered her desk when Missy asked permission to go to the jail.

"Yes. Check your room before you go, though."

Check her room? Had she left the bed unmade that morning? Didn't seem to matter much with Gwen gone. It was okay, though. She'd run in, chuck the sweatshirt she'd tied around her waist and make her bed. Taking two steps at a time, she dashed up the stairs and made a quick turn into her bedroom.

Gwen sat at the small desk, facing the door as if she'd been expecting her.

Missy gasped in surprise, crossed the room, and reached out to hug her. A swift warning in Gwen's eyes made her drop her arms back to her sides. Instead, she took a seat across from her tattooed roommate on her own bed.

Gwen said nothing. They sat for a moment in awkward silence. Missy always hated to start a conversation with Gwen, mostly because she sounded like a babbling idiot.

Finally, she blurted out the obvious. "How'd you get out?"

Gwen shrugged. "Don't know. Heard Mr. Wintroble dropped the charges."

"How did that happen?" Missy asked. Gwen hadn't stood a chance unless evidence had been found against Mr. Wintroble. What if someone who mattered actually believed Gwen and investigated?

Their school counselor was more than just creepy. Worse than a snake hiding under a rock and striking when disturbed, he'd positioned himself to strike for his own sick craziness.

What kind of shock waves would the truth about him send through the school? Most kids thought he was kind of strange, but harmless. What Mr. Wintroble did to Gwen proved he wasn't.

Missy thought about how she'd ducked for cover most of her life. And the times she'd decided to hide instead of face down a real enemy. Not Gwen, though.

Gwen knew Mr. Wintroble was a real threat. And she'd stood up to him. She'd punched out a man like a warrior defending her country, fighting for freedom. Missy'd never seen it until now.

Gwen was a champion.

True, she was sort of a champion in disguise. Missy would never have noticed her hero status if she hadn't been at the shelter, hadn't shared the same room.

Mr. Wintroble looked more and more like Mr. Lucas - good on the outside. Was that only because appearances got them what they wanted, no matter what it was?

Gwen finally spoke and broke into Missy's thoughts. "What you mean is that you can't figure out how *I'd* be the one let go after being assaulted by the high school counselor?"

Ouch. "Well. I mean, I'm sorry." Missy was already apologizing. This conversation wasn't going well.

She was right, though. Gwen was the one who'd been attacked and had acted in self-defense.

"I've been doing some investigating on my own since I got back," Gwen said, and pulled a piece of cloth from her pocket. "Thought you might be interested in this." She lay a crumpled piece of cloth on the table.

"A rag?"

"I found it hidden under the lilac bush. Smells like bleach. Has some red stains, like clay."

"Not blood?"

"No, dingbat. Somebody used it to wipe footprints off the window."

"Oh. You mean the night I saw somebody at Beatrice's window?"

"Reports of your lightning quick mind are greatly exaggerated," Gwen sneered.

Missy ignored the insult. She needed this information. "Do you know how someone got inside Bea's room, then disappeared before Adele or anyone else could find out who it was?"

"Only a theory. The runaways have all been from the shelter the last few months."

"I didn't know that." Once again, she was looking like a dimwit. But she had to know. Something inside told her Gwen held keys she needed. Missy just wasn't sure what they were.

"Somebody's selling those girls," Gwen said.

"Selling them?" Missy asked.

She sounded like she was two instead of fourteen. It was sad, but she couldn't explain, had no way to understand in her head what she knew in her heart. And that made her fall short in ways she hated. There was an adult world she knew nothing about. Like the word *molested* she'd heard Miss Terrell whisper to Adele. What did that mean?

Her heart told her it was like stealing something precious and irreplaceable. But that didn't mean she could explain it in words.

She and Pa'd never talked about sex. She'd guessed some things by listening to other girls, but that was pretty sketchy at best. Pa'd let her be a kid. Unlike Gwen who seemed ancient at the core.

Gwen rolled her eyes. "You're such an innocent." She stared at Missy with a mix of curiosity and…Was it envy? Missy felt a blush rise up from her neck to her head.

"Guess you can't help it," Gwen said.

If Missy opened her mouth right now, she'd prove her stupidity. She should understand these things. Except she was pretty sure there was a trade involved, like she'd have to give up something to get it. She didn't know much, but enough to figure out that Gwen'd been ripped off with no trade at all.

Gwen sighed, then sounded like she was trying to explain something to a child. "Look," she began. "Creeps who need a pretty girl without any strings attached. 'Cept there are strings. The ones tying up those girls and sending them down river. Not that you'll ever find the person behind it all. He'll be someone no one suspects."

"Down river?"

"River barges, shipping crates. Those girls are stuffed inside and sent to God knows where. Never heard from again."

"How do you know?"

"Remember Amelia who disappeared a few weeks back? She was asleep in the bed next to mine last time I saw her. When I woke up in the night, she was gone."

Gwen's fists clenched and her mouth drew into a tight line. "I ran outside to look for her 'cause we were friends. She'd have told me if she was leaving. I saw a cargo van, heard the door slam and watched it drive away. I ran after it, but it was too dark and they were going fast.

"There was this path I'd seen a couple of guys on before. Found out it led to the river. By the time I got there, somebody was loading a shipping crate on a barge. The same van was sitting on the county road above."

"Did you recognize the guys?"

"I know who they are, if that's what you mean." Gwen looked away, just as Missy hoped she'd tell her what she knew. Maybe she'd trust her. Just once.

Missy said the first thing that came to mind. "You know? Why haven't you called Sheriff Davis?"

"Look. This isn't story-time. It's bad stuff. The law

in this no-where town can't help." Gwen was closing down. She stood up as if she was done with Missy's company.

"But somebody's got to do something." Missy had to keep her talking. She needed help. Gwen couldn't shut her out now.

But she could. And did.

"Right," Gwen mocked, sighing in boredom. "And that something would be?"

"I don't know. I could, like—draw them to me. Kinda like bait?"

"Bait? Seriously?" Gwen rolled her eyes and snorted a laugh.

"It worked once. With Clarence."

"You *are* an innocent, aren't you?"

"Maybe we could work out a plan with Benjamin."

Gwen glared at her. "What makes you think anything *we* do would make a difference?"

"Miss Terrell helped you."

The instant the sentence came out of her mouth, Missy knew it was the wrong thing to say. Too late.

Gwen strode forward and into Missy's face. "Keep her out of this."

"That's not what I meant." Missy struggled to explain herself but knew she'd only dig a deeper hole. She felt the heat of Gwen's breath, the fear of her fury.

"Get out. Now." Gwen towered over Missy. She pointed at the door, short of shoving her out.

"But this is my room, too."

"Get out. Now."

Chapter 15

Missy got up and grabbed her backpack, staying alert for any sudden moves from Gwen. She went out into the hall and stifled a small groan. Once again, she'd screwed up. Gwen closed her heart for a good reason. What could Missy give her except ignorance?

She walked around the old Victorian house, trying to look inconspicuous. Had anyone else ever managed to get thrown out of a room at the shelter? Would any of the girls take her in? She could ask but was pretty sure she couldn't face another rejection in melt-down form.

It wasn't like she could go to Adele. Not after the fiasco with Beatrice and the intruder. Worse, it was too late to visit Pa. She'd have to see him tomorrow. Probably good, since being homeless hadn't been her plan for the day.

Missy headed to the back of the house where she remembered the back porch. Winding down the stairs and through the kitchen, she peered around to make sure no one saw her. She opened the screen door that led inside the porch, smelling dirt and a faint odor of pesticide. Hoes and rakes hung on the back wall. A spade and gardening gloves shoved inside an empty flower pot sat on a line of shelves. Missy checked the corners for spider webs and found a couple mouse traps instead.

The warm day turned cooler as the sun slipped from the horizon. It was time to get ready for dinner. Missy hid her backpack behind a bag of potting soil and ducked back into the kitchen, past a large pantry.

Adele led the charge in dinner preparations. Girls walked in and out of the kitchen to the dining room with plates, bowls and various stages of a meal. Missy's job was to help Beatrice set the table. Seemed simple enough, except for the daggers in Beatrice's eyes. A few of the girls with cooking privileges laughed and talked as they mashed potatoes and stirred gravy in the old cast iron skillet.

The chatter stopped when Missy came into the kitchen looking for more silverware. Silence. Another reminder that she didn't belong. After the meal was ready and the girls all gathered around the table, Gwen sat, refusing to look at Missy.

It was a long evening. Missy did her homework sitting on a worn velvet armchair, tucked away in the parlor no one ever visited. It was stuffy and the chairs were stiff and uncomfortable. And Missy felt like she should be dressed appropriately, which of course wasn't possible since she was born in a different century. No hoop skirts to be had in her closet.

Heavy curtains covered the windows like dusty shrouds. A walnut cabinet full of china stood along one of the walls. Missy pictured perfectly placed tea sets and porcelain cups held by perfectly lovely Southern ladies. She wondered what real life those parlor conversations had hidden.

After curfew, Missy took her backpack and snuck into the porch. The air was cool and damp, but not frigid. She found a tarp that Adele probably used to cover her azaleas during a cold snap and pulled the bag of potting soil off her backpack. Angling the bag to one corner of the porch, she covered it with the tarp.

Better than nothing. Missy curled up her legs, wrapped her arms around the backpack and covered herself with the rest of the tarp, then tried to sleep.

The din of insect symphonies came to life in the darkness. A hoot owl sounded in a tree beyond the house, calling its mate or signaling an attack. Every noise outside reminded her there was a whole world very much alive in darkness.

Part of that world took advantage of the cover of darkness, like Jeremiah Lucas and the thugs who obeyed his orders. She shivered and held her arms tighter around her body. At least she was sort of hidden by the tarp. She didn't have to worry about falling asleep and not hearing an intruder, though. She was wide awake.

Making sense of things was a lost cause at this point. She wondered how life had shoved both Gwen and Clarence into such a deep, lonely place. Could they be reached? By anyone?

She felt alone without Pa and at the shelter, but they'd been betrayed by people who were supposed to love them. No wonder neither of them walked down the halls with a smile and skip in their step. What a ninny she was for thinking they should, that either of them could pretend well enough that life was safe and good when it wasn't.

Missy woke up with a start. She could hear Adele banging things around in the kitchen, getting breakfast ready. How was she going to sneak out of the porch and into the kitchen? Especially looking like she'd slept there. She pulled fingers through her tangled hair and a piece of bark fell out. Where was she going to brush her teeth? And get changed? And go to the bathroom?

Her body was stiff from sleeping on the lumpy plastic bag. She took a minute to make a plan. One she hadn't made last night when she'd been in panic mode and rushed out of her room on pain of certain death. Now she needed to get ready for school without Adele seeing her sneak upstairs.

Missy waited until the kitchen became quiet. No more clash of plates being rinsed and placed in the dishwasher, no more mumble of morning voices and Adele's orders voiced through the din. She snuck a peek out of the curtained window of the door that led inside the kitchen. No one around.

Opening the door, she slipped out into the kitchen and saw a bowl of fruit on the counter. She grabbed an apple and banana, then sprinted up the stairs, watching to make sure no one saw her.

The good news was that she'd missed everyone. The bad news was she was late for school. The bus had already left. Missy grabbed clean clothes and her cosmetic bag and headed to the shower. Standing in the warm shower, the aches in her muscles quieted and she felt the muck of sleeping on top of a bag of potting soil wash away.

At school, the hallways were buzzing with stories about Gwen. Allison tossed her blonde hair and turned to her small horde of followers.

"I heard she busted her way out of jail. On the lam, so to speak."

Missy rolled her eyes and kept walking. She'd been thinking about their conversation. Gwen had said she knew who'd kidnapped her friend, who was behind the girls' disappearances. But she wasn't talking. And now she was nowhere in sight.

Clarence walked by as she was closing her locker at the end of the day. He looked straight ahead, as if suddenly she'd turned invisible. Or that he hoped she had, anyway. He probably tasted river water every time he saw her.

She needed to get back into the Lucas house, but how could she? Clarence sure wasn't going to help and she couldn't face Mr. Lucas one more time on his turf. Chances were good she'd never make it out again.

After school she rode down the county road until a circle of trees appeared. The grove was close enough to see the river through its cover, but still near the road. A perfect place to think. She'd checked for snakes and settled herself under a tree when a navy-blue Lincoln sped by, heading south on the county road. It was Mr. Lucas.

There weren't many options in that direction. The only major road out of town, it was the fastest route to Jackson. It was a gamble, but maybe she'd have time to carry out a plan. Jumping back on her bike, she headed toward town.

She was nuts to go back into that house, even with Mr. Lucas out of the way. Still, she needed more clues and there was only one way to find them. She'd have to figure out an excuse to talk to Clarence.

Mama'd taught her since she was little to respect people's privacy. For sure not to go opening doors and closets on a quest in somebody else's house. Even in their house, she stood at a closet door and pointed at Missy, *No snooping*.

She'd tucked early birthday and Christmas presents inside and didn't want Missy to see them ahead of time. Sometimes the urge to uncover treasure overcame all the good Mama'd tried to impart. Got whooped a time or two for it.

It was worth it. She'd never grown out of that longing to know the truth behind secrets.

Now it wasn't about hidden gifts. It was about fearing what and who waited to rise up and grab her.

How would a conversation with Clarence work? Like the one she'd tried to have with Gwen? She didn't want to think about that. He'd bullied her for years. She'd watched him bullied after the snare incident. Maybe she could make things right, as right as she could manage, anyway. And see if he'd tell her anything about his dad.

It was lame, but she'd pretend like she had extra tickets to the school play. Some kids had been pawning them off in speech class. She'd taken a few even though there was no way she'd go to any stupid play.

Pulling into the driveway of the Lucas home, she stashed her bike near a tree by the street. It'd be ready if she needed a fast getaway. She rang the doorbell, looking behind and all around, on high alert. She was about to run when the heavy door opened and Clarence stood there alone.

"Hey, Clarence."

He didn't say anything but didn't shut the door in her face.

"Umm, would you like to buy a couple tickets to the school play? Or, actually, I'll give them to you, if you're interested."

She was a pitiful excuse for a liar and they both

knew it. Clarence stared back, his face expressionless, his eyes unreadable. She stood, holding a couple red tickets in front of her as if she offered chocolate to a two-year old.

In the awkward silence she wondered if he had any friends to hang out with after school, or shoot hoops with or go to a movie. No one she'd ever seen.

Clarence finally spoke. "Want to come in?"

Missy paused. It wasn't too late. She could turn and leave. But she had to see inside that house one more time. She nodded and walked across the threshold into the same foyer, with the same closet facing her. Was the hat still there? Clarence didn't seem to notice and walked into the kitchen.

Missy'd never really looked around the house. She peeked into a living room beyond the kitchen. A towering floral arrangement perched on a grand piano. But no pictures of Clarence as a toddler, laughing as his dad caught him mid-flight or posed next to his little sister with a protective arm around her.

The kitchen was spotless. Missy thought about their catch-all kitchen counter, full of keys, homework, mail waiting to be opened and more to be tossed. It got to be a mountain sometimes. But it was proof they lived there.

She couldn't imagine cookies coming from that oven. Or crumbs on the perfectly waxed floor. Ivory silk curtains lined the windows, with the tiniest slump in their perfect drape to hardwood floors.

They sat down at the counter, right across from the drawer and red binder inside.

"Want something to drink?

"Sure." She had no idea what he'd offer. Potion of

rat's tail and salamander slime? Without a plan coming to mind, she looked around the kitchen and noticed a tiny framed picture tucked away behind a bowl of artificial fruit on the counter. An attractive lady in a yellow dress smiled like a beauty queen at an unseen photographer.

"Is that a picture of your mom?"

Clarence looked at the picture and nodded.

"She's really pretty."

Clarence turned to pull milk and chocolate syrup out of the refrigerator. As she peeked inside, she saw even the refrigerator was clean. Missy wondered who did the shopping. Or if anyone else had been invited into the kitchen.

"She loved that dress," he said, as he reached for two glasses from a nearby cabinet.

He hadn't ignored her after all. It seemed like sort of a disconnected way to answer a compliment about his mom. Then again, what would she say if he asked about a picture of her mom? That was a lot to sum up in one sentence.

"The last time I saw her a seam had unraveled on one shoulder," he said. "Not like her to wear anything less than perfect."

Clarence filled the glasses with milk, then squirted chocolate in each one. Missy watched globs of chocolate sauce descend in waves and sink to the bottom the glasses. Opening a drawer under the counter, Clarence brought out two spoons and laid them beside the glasses.

Missy picked hers up and gently rotated the spoon against the bottom of the cup. Clarence rattled his spoon against the glass, pulled it out and gulped the milk, then wiped his face with one arm.

He glanced back at the picture, then to the empty glass. "Couldn't remember the last time she'd said a word. Then one day I came home and she was gone. Guess she got what she wanted. A life without me."

What could she say? For once, his meanness made a little sense. How would it feel to miss your mama and know she left on purpose? And that somehow it was your fault? Missy didn't want to understand, but she did.

She knew about coming up short in all the wrong ways. It hadn't been hard to figure out after the accident. She wasn't allowed to snuggle anymore and couldn't rush in for a morning kiss. Mama's door was closed, even though Missy needed to show her the first crocus broken through cool earth.

The phone rang, interrupting the silence. Clarence answered. "Lucas residence." He listened without response, then hung up the receiver. "I gotta leave." He looked straight ahead, the edges around his eyes frantic.

"That's okay. I'll let myself out the front door. See you at school?"

Clarence didn't answer. He walked in long strides to the back door and slammed it behind him.

What message in that call made him rush out the back? She opened the front door and looked around. The smart thing to do was to jump on her bike and ride away. But being rational wouldn't tell her what she needed to know. She walked back inside, leaving the door ajar.

She needed to check out that binder in the kitchen drawer. There were probably other files in an office upstairs, but making that trek was too dangerous.

Besides, it had looked like some kind of file and this kitchen wasn't the kind for a stash of favorite recipes. The ones Mama left behind were dogeared and oil-stained, with sticky spots still intact. It wouldn't take long just to take a peek.

The drawer felt like a million miles away, but she crept toward it with an eye on the front door. Reaching inside, she pulled out the binder and opened it.

Inside were laminated newspaper clippings. The headline of the first article blared LOCAL GIRL MISSING and included an interview with a distraught mom. Amelia's school picture with her wan smile and porcelain features was next to it.

The second was about Danielle Sommers. It made the front page, too. She flipped through page after page of articles about runaway girls, carefully cut out and placed in order. Unlike a family photo album, this one chronicled grief and loss. And each story was cloaked in unanswered questions.

Missy scanned the pages, searching, and listening at the same time for anyone's approach. Finally, she found what she was looking for.

MURDER AT THE HOMOCHITTO RIVER. It was the report on Ephraim's murder.

What had Gwen said? That no one ever saw the person behind the kidnappings? That he stayed apart from the dirty work and used others to carry out his plan? Was it a man like Jeremiah Lucas, who kept meticulous records on every runaway, as well as Ephraim's murder?

Missy heard the low hum and crunch of loose gravel as a car pulled into the driveway. Then the screech of the garage door being opened. Her hand trembled as she closed the drawer. It slipped in her hand and made a sickening thud as she turned to run.

One, two, three steps… How many would it take to reach what she could see right ahead? Would she make it at all?

Finally, she reached the back door. The doorknob stuck as if it were locked. Adrenaline surged inside and heat rose from her gut to her head. Before long she'd be out cold on the floor, like she'd been in Mr. Lucas' office months before.

Dizzy with fear, she tried again.

The door sprung open on her next try, and she slipped outside. Drinking in the fresh air, she took another deep breath and closed the door with a click.

She plunged her body forward, running toward the neighbor's garden, then remembered her bike. Circling around the back of the garden, she walked to the sidewalk, imagining herself wearing concrete boots. Anything to slow her down long enough to pretend all was well. The Lucas home towered above as she walked its sidewalk, with her eye on the bike in front of her. She pulled it from the trunk it rested against and climbed on, her limbs weak and mushy. With a long breath, she heaved herself forward into the street and looked behind as she rode away.

Jeremiah Lucas stood at the living room window, curtains in hand.

Chapter 16

A cool breeze blew over a hollow filled with river birch. The birch leaves, new with winter's shift to spring, fluttered like slender fingers in soft applause. The river meandered in the distance, even though she couldn't see it. That was good. The county road was close enough for a quick escape if she needed one, but she was hidden from its traffic.

She sat under the canopy of branches and rested her head against her knees. What to do? The weight of what she knew pressed on her chest. Her breath came in erratic spurts in between gulps for air. She had to sort things out in her head about the notebook.

Articles in perfect order, neatly cut and preserved on every runaway. And on Ephraim's murder. It was like a memory book of nightmares. Was Mr. Lucas keeping the binder for his own information as an attorney? Or for the fiendish pleasure of seeing his evil work in print?

And who could she tell? Sheriff Davis had no reason to believe her over Jeremiah Lucas. Neither did Adele. Jeremiah Lucas was still considered a pillar of the community by anyone who mattered. Miss Terrell seemed nice and had reached out to Gwen. But what help could a past beauty queen offer against someone like Mr. Lucas?

No available adults. Okay. Maybe…she could form

a team of friends. But who would they be?

Benjamin was the only one, other than her, who knew she'd found the rainhat in Mr. Lucas' closet. Now there was more. Much more. His catapult had shut down the school bully, but Mr. Lucas was a king pin behind an evil far too big to dangle over the river. Gwen was like a simmering volcano with puffs of smoke and tremors wherever she went. But who else did she have, anyway?

Missy sighed and rode back to the shelter. A wall clock chimed nine o'clock and all she could hear was quiet stirrings inside each room. She was tired of sleeping on the back porch, but she needed time alone to think. She didn't have the strength to keep her guard up, knowing nowhere was safe anymore.

She stared up into the night sky and tried to sort things out. She and Mama had stretched out together on summer nights, peering into the dark expanse lit by tiny patterns of light. They'd found Polaris, at the tail end of Ursa Minor, the little bear. The North Star always had its eye on the cub, just like she and Pa looked out for her.

So far away, so long ago. But it was the same sky, the same stars. Stars wouldn't be much help with what she'd found today, though. She needed some flesh and blood help. And more information. Maybe she could get Benjamin and Gwen to meet her after school at the grove of trees right off the county road.

They could work out some sort of plan. She had to have something, couldn't pretend she didn't know what she'd witnessed in the Lucas home.

She fell into a deep sleep and woke up again to a noisy kitchen. Her tardies were building up. Without any pride left, she'd beg Gwen to let her back in their room. Maybe Gwen would take pity on her sorry self.

The morning shone like a promise of summer days ahead on her ride to school. She slipped a note to Benjamin as he walked by and stashed another in Gwen's locker. *Meet me by the birch trees at the hollow after school. Missy*

Clarence walked by as she stuffed the note in Gwen's locker. He nodded and then kept walking. Missy shrugged off a surge of anxiety. He didn't need to know any of this, but how would he find out about the meeting? She sure wasn't telling him.

The school day moved like muddy sludge, every class longer, and with every hour her heart pounded faster. When the last bell rang, she charged out of school, got on her bike and pedaled down the highway on the way to a circle of birch trees. She hid her bike behind one tree, resting it against its trunk. She could grab it and pedal away if she needed to. Benjamin was first to arrive.

"You shot out of school like somebody was after you." He stopped himself, realizing what he'd said. "Sorry. What's going on?"

She shrugged. "I invited Gwen to meet us here."

"Because…"

"She needs to know what I saw at Mr. Lucas' house. She's been living at the shelter for a while. Don't know for sure how long, but long enough to know something that might help."

Missy didn't mention that she'd been booted out of her room. What could Benjamin do about it, anyway? If she mentioned it to him and it got back to Gwen, that would only confirm her weakling status.

"What you saw at Mr. Lucas' house?" Benjamin asked. "You mean the rainhat in the closet?"

"I went to see Clarence yesterday."

"You're kidding." Benjamin's eyebrows rose, and he crossed his arms over his chest.

"I felt like he might know something. That maybe...Well, maybe he isn't an enemy."

"Right. The son of Jeremiah Lucas. What makes you think he'd be any different?"

Missy kept talking, ignoring his protests. "Mr. Lucas wasn't there. Clarence asked me to come inside."

"In the house? What were you thinking?"

"I needed to say I was sorry." Missy popped down onto the grass. It was hard to explain to someone like Benjamin. He was kindness to the core—except when it came to Clarence. When Clarence had slammed him against a wall of lockers at school, he didn't retaliate. But when Clarence came against her? Benjamin had shifted the catapult into a bully-defying machine.

How weird that she fell without warning into a friend like Benjamin. How was it even possible? She looked at him and smiled. Benjamin looked back confused.

"What?"

"You," she said.

"What about me?"

"Look, I know I'm pretty certifiably crazy." Her eyes teared up and spilled over. Benjamin fingered a long strand of hair and touched her cheek. Missy tried not to get distracted. Whatever that meant. How could she think with all this never-before-felt kind of stuff stirring in her belly, filtering her eyes, filling her heart?

"Anyway, I needed to know some things.

Clarence's house had the clues I needed. And...

"I was wrong for the way I treated him. There's something terrible in his house, in his dad. What would it be like if home wasn't safe? If it was like a giant Venus flytrap that sucks you in and makes you die a slow death in its poison? That's what I saw over there. Can't explain it all. I found more than I wanted to."

Benjamin nodded. "Go ahead."

Missy leaned closer. "Clarence told me some really sad stuff about his mom. I was hoping he'd tell me something about...well, I don't know. Something, anything about his dad. But then he got a phone call and ran out. I told him I'd go out the front but stayed to check this notebook I'd seen before in one of the kitchen drawers.

"There were all these newspaper clippings about the runaways, even the one about Ephraim's murder." Missy stopped to take a breath. "Why would he keep all those?" she asked.

Benjamin didn't say anything. He was thinking and couldn't be reached for a response. He did that at school, too. That was one reason she'd thought he was stuck-up. Now she knew he was just inhabiting another world in his brain. One she couldn't always reach. She'd try, anyway.

"Do you think Mr. Lucas has something to do with the runaways, too? Are the runaways and Ephraim's murder connected?"

Benjamin still didn't have anything to say. Missy saw Gwen slouch down the hill from the county road above. She walked past them both and stood under a tree with her arms folded.

"Hey, Gwen," said Missy. A greeting couldn't hurt.

After all, she had shown up and Missy knew that meant something. What, she wasn't sure.

"Hey, yourself. What's going on?" she asked.

Other than her back hurt and her hair smelled like potting soil, she was fine. But now wasn't the time for that discussion.

"I found something at Mr. Lucas' house," Missy started. "It was a notebook full of articles about the runaways. Even one about Ephraim's murder. Don't know what it means, except maybe Mr. Lucas is involved." She stopped and waited for Gwen to respond.

A noise rustled in the brush behind them. Maybe it was a rabbit. They were too far away from the marsh grass for it to be a snake. She hoped, anyway.

Gwen didn't have anything to say. She sat back on her heels and leaned against the tree. Missy didn't know where to go from here. She didn't want to be the one who made the plan. But neither Gwen nor Benjamin were contributing at this point.

"Look, we could make a plan," she said. "Meet here some afternoon, see if…"

Missy heard what sounded like a stick breaking as someone walked the path. Gwen stood up and looked around. "Who's out there?" she demanded.

Missy turned around to see Clarence trip over a root and stumble into the clearing. His face was red. He looked embarrassed. And mad.

What had he heard? How long had he been hiding?

"What are you doing here, Creepo?" asked Gwen.

"What about you, Neutron Jane?"

Gwen stiffened. Missy tried to smile. "Hey, Clarence," said Missy. "What's goin' on?"

Clarence just glared at her, but she saw hurt hiding in his eyes. Had he heard her talking about his dad?

"Look, you weren't invited to this party. Shove off," said Gwen.

"Wasn't lookin' for a party."

Missy wondered what he *had* been looking for.

Gwen stalked to Clarence and stood with her hands on her hips, fists clenched. The volcano was ready to blow. But Clarence had her on size. She looked like a Chihuahua facing down a Rottweiler.

Benjamin stood between them like a wedge in a door. "Look, we're here to talk about a plan. Either settle down or leave."

"What kind of plan?" asked Clarence.

"None of your business," snarled Gwen.

"Look, we're trying to figure out what's been going on with the runaways," said Missy.

"Runaways? You mean the ones they've been playing up in the Podunk *Gazette*? There ain't nothing wrong with any of them. Can't nobody prove they've done anything but high-tailed it out of this stupid town. Anything else is just fodder for the local news. Have to drum up something other than some dork grandmother jaywalking across Main Street.

"Besides, we care why? They're all rejects, anyway," said Clarence.

"Good time for this meeting to end," said Gwen. She turned away from Clarence and stalked away, charging back up the hill to the county road.

So much for help. Missy wondered if Gwen'd sized him up and decided he wasn't worth the challenge. It wasn't like her to back down from a good fight.

Missy turned to see Clarence leaving down the

path where he'd come.

She didn't know whether to yell back to him, apologize, or ignore the fact he'd probably heard her accuse his dad of being behind the runaways. And what about that path? He'd been able to sneak up on them, well, as much as a two-hundred pound fourteen-year-old could sneak.

Gwen had talked about a path she'd seen that led to the river. One where barges waited. She'd have to check this one out.

"What was that all about?" she asked, walking to the tree where Benjamin stood.

He plopped down on the ground and patted the earth beside him. "Pull up a chair." Missy looked around for critters, then sat down.

"So?" Missy asked.

"He likes you."

"No." Missy rose up off the ground and looked back toward the path. "He hates me.

"He makes that clear every time I see him. Except for today."

Benjamin continued like he hadn't heard what she said. "He probably followed you after school."

"That's creepy. Why would he do that?"

Benjamin stopped and stared at her. She squirmed under his gaze. Had she forgotten to brush her teeth that morning? She pulled on her jeans and straightened her T-shirt, like something had to be wrong or missing. She always forgot to check herself in the mirror before rushing out for the day.

"You listened to him," he answered.

"What?" Benjamin had this secret code going on in his mind. She wasn't sure how it worked. Still, with

Benjamin it was worth staying close just to figure it out.

"Who's ever really listened to Clarence," he said, "or talked to him like a friend?"

"Nobody," said Missy. "Even if they tried, he'd find a way to make them sorry they did."

"Right. Except, he told you things he hasn't told anybody else. How do you think he'd feel with a beautiful girl coming over just to be nice?"

"Beautiful? Can't count the times he's called me ugly."

"It's just that..." Benjamin stopped and blushed. "Well, you're..."

Missy didn't know what to say. "I'm what?"

"You're...special."

"That's what they always say about losers."

"Quit being a brat and listen," he said. "You were nice to Clarence. And he wanted to see if, well, if you'd be a friend the next day after what he told you. No wonder he was so mad. You were talking about his dad. He felt betrayed."

How did she know Clarence was listening in? Listening to Benjamin proved she was clueless. As usual. "What should we do?"

Benjamin shrugged his shoulders. "Just because he likes you doesn't mean we can trust him. I mean, Mr. Lucas is his dad."

"Maybe he doesn't know what's going on."

"Hard to believe," he said. A hawk screeched overhead, on the hunt or on the alert. What was Clarence? Predator or prey? Missy turned back to Benjamin. He was peering at an ant on the ground. "Still, any kind of dad is hard to turn your back on."

Missy watched a tiny look of loss creep in around

his eyes. She recognized that look. He missed his dad. She didn't know for sure what happened, only that he was gone.

She wondered what he remembered. Her memories had dwindled into an odd combination of scents and images she wasn't even sure were real. It had been so long, and she'd fought so hard to recall everything about Mama. Losing those memories were like a final blow.

Memories were sacred ground. She wasn't sure if she was invited into that place Benjamin had kept for him and his dad.

"What?" Benjamin had turned away for an instant, then returned his gaze to her.

Missy stumbled with her words. "I was thinking about your dad. Do you remember…"

He pulled his legs close and wrapped his arms around them, then spoke in a soft voice. "He made me laugh."

Missy scooted closer to him. Benjamin smiled. "You might be a little like him."

"Me?"

"Fun. Not boring. 'Course, I don't remember much. We wrestled and he let me win. You, on the other hand, would never let me win." He poked her in the arm. "He whispered a Shabbat blessing in my ear every week. *The Lord bless and keep you. May His face shine upon you and give you peace.*"

The bigness of his loss and the confusion over Clarence overtook Missy. She buried her head in her arms and sobbed. Benjamin drew his arm around her. They didn't say anything, just sat until the sun started its descent and it was time to get back to the shelter.

Benjamin turned to her, hugged her tightly and said, "Thanks."

Missy pulled closer. "Don't leave." She sat a little longer, then spoke. "I've been thinking about this plan. It's kind of a long shot. We've used it once before."

"Once before?" asked Benjamin. "How so?"

"What if I'm the bait?" she asked

Chapter 17

Benjamin stared at her with his *Are you crazy?* look.

"You know, like I was for Clarence. Minus the disaster at the end where we both almost drowned. We could meet tomorrow night, right here. And figure out a plan."

Benjamin opened his mouth, then shut it. "No. No way. It's too dangerous."

It was Missy's turn to be lost in thought. She finally spoke. "There's something in Clarence that wants a way out."

"Evidence?"

"Mr. Lucas could've carted me off somewhere that day when he knew I'd seen the rainhat, but when Clarence showed up he didn't help his dad. I'd have been just another one of those girls who disappeared. What if he wants to change? Wants to do right?"

"I can't take that chance."

Missy peeked over her knees and looked at his eyes. Was he for real? Did he really care?

"What?" he asked.

"I, well, I mean you're..."

"As good looking as David Cassidy?"

Missy blushed. He leaned over, one arm around her shoulder, aiming for her lips. Missy keeled over and they both landed on the soft earth. Missy tried to sit up at the same time Benjamin leaned in. Her arm caught his lower jaw in an upward jab. "Oww!"

"Sorry!"

Missy was mortified, but Benjamin leaned against the tree and laughed.

"Let's try this again." Benjamin pinned her arms to her side with his, then kissed her. Missy shut her eyes and felt the warm press of his lips against hers. He pulled her closer.

His breath mixed up with hers, and she smelled a hint of peanut butter. Every cell in her body was on high alert. How was she supposed to breathe during a kiss, anyway? She pulled away and took a deep breath.

Would she pass out? At least she was in good hands. Benjamin leaned in again. This time, she relaxed in his arms.

Somehow, she felt safe.

Her heart still raced, but now it was because she felt perched on top of a waterfall on a hot summer afternoon. Her body shivered as his kiss lingered and arms pressed her to his chest.

The sound of gravel crunching startled her, and she jerked upright, knocking Benjamin over, then saw dust and heard gravel crackle again as the car pulled back onto the highway.

Benjamin's face flushed a bright red. He leaned against the tree and tried to re-tuck his shirttail. She stood, perched on her bike. Neither looked into the other one's eyes.

She'd been caught up in something strong, like a whirlpool's swirl. After an awkward silence, Benjamin grinned. "That was nice."

Missy nodded and then laughed with a snort.

They'd stepped out of the crush of Ephraim's murder and the notebook of terrors for a while. Suddenly, she felt shy. Benjamin pulled a hand through his hair and looked at his watch.

"You gotta go? Can we meet here tomorrow? Make a plan?" Missy asked.

"Yep. Mom's got company coming." Benjamin fidgeted with his bike handles, turning them this way and that. Finally, he blurted out, "I know you're gonna be mad. But I'm just going to say it.

"We need to call Sheriff Davis. Tell him what you know."

Missy looked at him like she'd been slapped. Benjamin backed away. "I'm not kidding," he said.

Fire rose up in Missy's belly. He didn't understand after all. She'd already hold him how she felt about Sheriff Davis. He didn't care.

"What?" Benjamin looked confused.

"Leave me alone." She turned and charged toward her bike.

"Why?"

She turned and pointed her finger at him, her body shaking against her will. Why was she always so weak? Betrayal, anger, plus something she couldn't name rose up out of her voice. "I told you. He's the one who arrested Pa. I hate that sorry excuse for an officer of the law."

"Right. That's a great reason to go with an idiot plan."

Missy stood frozen, her finger still pointing. *Idiot plan.* So, that's what he thought.

"I didn't call *you* an idiot," he said, sounding like he was back pedaling. "Your plan is without reason, full of holes, and…"

Missy pulled her bike upright and steered it up the bank.

"Missy. Stop."

But she was already on her bike, headed back to the shelter.

Idiot, idiot, idiot bounced back and forth in her brain. She'd almost opened her heart. She'd been crazy all right, crazy with fear and willing to trust anybody.

Benjamin called her name a couple more times, but she refused to look back. Zigzagging around another route back to the shelter, she lost him. She tried to swallow a big lump in her throat, but it caught somewhere between her heart and mouth.

He thought he was so smart. Smart enough to figure out she wasn't in his league. Worst of all, he didn't even care that her dad was stuck in jail, an innocent man. All because of Sheriff Davis.

So much for a friend. She'd almost believed he cared.

She'd done it before; she'd do it again. She'd check Benjamin out of the door of her heart without a backward glance.

Not that it wouldn't hurt at first. But the hurt would go away, especially when the hardness set in. She'd find more evidence against him. She'd prove to herself he'd only looked like a friend.

It wouldn't take long.

She hoped.

The angle of the sun reached deep into the horizon. She was late for dinner. The closer she got, the more she knew she couldn't face anyone, much less the girls at the shelter with their cold stares and silence. Pulling off the county road, Missy climbed a big tree by the school that overlooked the river and curled herself in the giant crook of one branch.

She was alone. Again. Seemed like life kept pulling her to an abandoned place. Maybe that was the way it was supposed to be. Maybe asking for help was only another way to admit that she was stupid. Not even capable of helping her dad.

So she'd found out Mr. Lucas might be behind the missing girls. What good was that? She had no proof that would stick against a guy considered a pillar of Avalon society. Maybe the girls *had* just run off.

But what if someone was hurting them? And she knew and did nothing about it? Her heart ached too much to sit still for long. She had to figure out a plan, whether she knew how or not.

The rough bark jabbed her back. She wiggled against it, but her legs were restless and cramped. Her legs had gotten so long she couldn't get them situated along the dense foliage. A spider ambled over its web on an outer branch. One too many spiders for her.

Missy shimmied down branch by branch until her feet thudded to the ground. A cool breeze shifted branches and rustled leaves. It was a simple decision.

She'd check out that path and see if it led to the river, like the one Gwen had talked about. What were the chances it was the same path? There were countless places that led to the river from that county road. A search might not even matter. But she had to move anyway, and that direction was as good as any.

Sunlight faded into dusk as she circled around to the grove of trees where she and Benjamin had met less than an hour ago. There was a speed limit sign on the road beside it. Missy parked her bike behind the same tree and saw the path just beyond a patch of river grass.

She tripped on a root, steadied herself and followed the path downhill. The rustle of water flowing signaled the river before it came into view. Hiding behind a tree, she peered out at the rushing current below.

A barge sat alone on the pebbled shore. Gwen had talked about seeing a barge the night her friend was kidnapped. She stayed a moment longer, searching the perimeter. The sky had lost its peachy haze and a lone streetlight beckoned from a residential area beyond the road. She was really late now, and probably in trouble with Adele.

Hiking up the path, she found her bike and rode back in the twilight. She parked her bike under a bush and headed inside. Adele gave her a steely-eyed gaze as Missy explained she'd lost track of time and was sorry she was late.

"Don't let it happen again. There are leftovers in the frig if you're hungry." Adele turned and headed to her room to watch T.V. Lucky for Missy, it was Thursday night and time for *Perry Mason*.

Missy'd dodged a bullet and knew it. She headed to the kitchen as if she was going to eat but checked out the porch instead. The potting soil and tarp were still there, waiting for her. Something inside her rose up.

She wasn't sleeping on the back porch one more night. Since Gwen had shown up at the river, maybe it was okay to test the waters. If she was in another nasty mood, Missy'd figure that out pretty quick. Taking off her shoes, she crept upstairs, avoiding the creaky slats in the wood floor. She peeked inside the bedroom, prepared to run if something was hurled in her direction.

Gwen's bed was empty. Her backpack was there, tumbled over on the floor. A pair of jeans lay on the unrumpled bedspread. But no Gwen. Where could she be after curfew?

Missy looked around for a note or any evidence she'd left behind. Nothing. Maybe she was in somebody else's room. That was against the rules, but then again, so was throwing out her roommate.

She grabbed her flashlight and walked back into the quiet hall, looking at each door and finding them closed. She went back downstairs to Adele's room where she'd heard murmurs of the television. All was quiet.

She was worried over nothing. After making the trek back up the stairs and to her room, Missy sat on the bed, rocking back and forth. The unrest in her belly wouldn't go away.

She got up and tiptoed downstairs again. Moonlight shone through the kitchen window as she made her way back to Adele's room.

"Adele," she whispered and knocked quietly on the door.

No answer.

She knocked louder again. Still no answer. Something was wrong. It wasn't like Adele to sleep so soundly.

Missy tried to think of someone Gwen had hung out with at the shelter. No one came to mind. Most of the girls kept their distance, watching her with a wary eye. Still, she had to make sure Gwen was okay.

Then again, if Gwen wasn't at the shelter, that meant she'd have to go out into the darkness and look

Lord knew where for someone who didn't even like her.

Why should she care? She'd slept bunched up on a bag of potting soil, listening to the call of a hoot owl all week and looking toward the back door, hoping the lock held against whatever the night might let creep in. Her back ached and she longed for a real bed with a real pillow. Even if it *was* at the shelter.

One thought tormented her.

What if Jeremiah Lucas had sent someone after her and found Gwen instead? Not that Gwen couldn't defend herself, but his kind of meanness was way bigger than a sixteen-year old's pent-up rage. She'd only be another victim in a long list of others.

That meant Missy had to do something, had to go back into the darkness.

But no, she couldn't. Not again.

She thought back to that night at the river when she'd watched a mob kill an innocent man. All she knew and loved had spiraled into chaos from that moment, in the hands of something more evil than she'd ever known.

Evil that had always been there but was only covered up.

She'd been the one who'd uncovered it.

A memory rose up like an anaconda of another day when she was eight-years old. The time she'd forgotten to meet Mama at the spring.

She'd promised. She'd be there with the cookies, ready for their picnic in the grove of trees on a high ridge overlooking the river. A bubbling spring nearby made it their favorite refuge. But she'd been in the middle of a book and forgotten the time.

When Mama'd fallen, she wasn't there. Pa'd brought her back to the house, slumped in his arms and unconscious. She'd died weeks later. The impact had broken something inside her already frail body.

Forgetting had cost her mama. And a vow she'd made to never forget again had pulled her out on a rainy summer night only to discover something terrible, something Jeremiah Lucas hoped would remain unseen.

That secret was like a nest of copperheads, growing and gaining strength. The question wasn't if Lucas would strike. It was where and when.

Why should she venture back out into the night to find Gwen? She couldn't save everyone. Who was she to think that she could?

Except Gwen had been there, right in her path. If all this mess hadn't happened, she wouldn't have met her. Would barely have known the shelter even existed, much less cared about the girls who lived there.

Had God somehow been behind that?

Missy hadn't thought about God much since Mama died. Somehow the hope that He was there listening had plunged deep into the hurt and refused to surface.

She'd take her flashlight and bike back to the path. The streetlights would light the way. Sort of.

Nothing in Missy wanted to go into the night. But she'd hurry, check the path, and come right back. It wouldn't take long. She tied on her shoes and dashed out the door before she could change her mind. Then did an about-face on her way out to retrieve the old pocket knife tucked away in the weathered chest of drawers she and Gwen shared.

Tiptoeing down the stairs, she looked this way and that, opened the front door with a tiny screech, and headed outside. The call of a nighthawk sounded near a line of trees beside the road. Streetlights cast circular hoops on the sidewalk, and the moon shone full overhead.

She stood on the porch, tempted to go back inside. She had no idea what she'd do when she got to the path. Maybe she'd figure it out along the way. She pointed her bike toward the route back to the county road that ran parallel to the river. Streetlights faded as she pedaled away from the residential area of Avalon.

Turning on her flashlight, she held it in front of her, hoping it would act as a small headlight. Its beam jiggled up and down in her hand as she rode. Such a tiny attempt to bring light into darkness. Seemed kinda poetic. Not now, though, when she was scared spitless and could barely breathe through the fear that kept shouting, *go back to the shelter, stupid.*

The moon helped as it cast its dim light around the sleeping town. As long as she didn't think too much about the shadows that moved as she rode, she was okay. This was a good time to turn off her imagination.

She passed the school and found the county road. There were a few security lights around the playground, but they faded as she rode further away. Not much traffic right now, although she ducked off the road and behind a thicket of bushes when a pick-up truck lumbered by.

Back on her bike, Missy kept riding forward. Within minutes, the tiny shaft of light illuminated a speed limit sign. It was the landmark she'd remembered.

Ditching her bike under a tree out of sight from the road, she picked through underbrush. A soft breeze swirled through the trees, and she crept into the open area. The path had to be close by. She tripped on a root that extended out of the soil and fell headfirst, flinging the flashlight into a crazy arc on impacted ground.

After brushing off leaves and dirt, she rubbed her throbbing knees. Guess that was one way to find the path.

The flashlight beamed like a small sentinel. Cicadas roared around her, and a bird swooped down in front of her. Not a bird, she reminded herself. It was a bat. She could back out now, return to the shelter, and figure she'd done all she could. If not, it was time to turn off the flashlight. She grabbed it and pressed the plastic until the light extinguished. New tremors of panic shot through her body.

The rush of the river grew louder as she crept down the path, feeling her way downhill. She grabbed one tree, then another, for support and potential cover. Before long, lights bobbed near what looked like a barge tethered by the shoreline. In the distance, the sound of a vehicle pulled off asphalt and onto gravel nearby. She crouched lower.

It was hard to make out details in the darkness, and she didn't dare turn on her flashlight. Her skin was cool and clammy despite the warm spring night, and her breathing had shifted into warp speed. If she didn't leave now, she'd be in a puddle on the ground, open to whatever darkness invited. Pulling in a deep breath, she made the decision. It was time to go before she passed out.

As she turned to leave, a shadow crossed the path ahead. With one lunge, the shadow became a man in black sweats and mask.

Strong arms yanked her body backwards and covered her mouth.

Chapter 18

Like a wild animal caught in a snare, Missy kicked and writhed with all her strength. She broke free and ran. The man lunged forward and grabbed her hair. He jerked her around and slapped her hard.

Her jaw shifted and hot pain shot through her face. She screamed from her gut, forcing out the fear, shouting it down, making it go far, far from her.

But it didn't. A filthy hand descended over her mouth. She bit into the soft flesh of his palm, tasting earth, blood and a faint trace of oil. He roared, then smacked her with a blow that threw her to the ground. Kicking her with a heavy boot, he shoved her to her stomach where he stabbed one knee into her back and stuffed an oily rag in her mouth. Her body shrieked in pain, but she kept fighting until another kick smashed her side and she went limp.

It was done, she was his.

Missy felt her wrists bound first, then ankles. Sticky tape circled her head and covered her mouth. She couldn't breathe, couldn't gasp for air. She pulled in air through her nostrils as her heart pounded in the short staccatos she knew so well. Nausea flooded her belly and the world around her spun in tight, unrelenting circles. She tried to struggle, but her muscles wouldn't obey; tried to speak, but felt only the tape binding her mouth.

Like moving into the shadows, Missy's senses faded. A narrow strip of light as if from beneath a door grew smaller, then smaller. Then, like a shutter in the hands of an avowed recluse, it slammed shut and she was gone.

****

It was her sense of hearing that returned first. Someone coughed nearby. She struggled to see, but scratchy fibers covered her eyes. Cold metal seeped through her bones and she shivered. Pain shot through her body when she tried to sit up. The tug of ropes that bound her hands and ankles burned raw flesh.

Her mouth was still bound. She had no voice, no way to move, to go back, to change her mind. It was too late. They'd gotten the one they wanted.

Her.

Tears soaked what felt like a stocking cap. It was hard to breathe. She wiggled her nose, then shifted her head back and forth to free it. When she felt close to passing out again, a hand pulled the hat away from her nostrils. She wanted to reach up and touch it. It wasn't the hand that had slapped and hurled her to the ground.

A sudden stop hurtled her into what felt like a wheel well. The impact banged her knees and knocked her breathless. She must be in a van. She heard a door rattling with the motion of the vehicle. They were moving fast, too fast to bail, even if she could.

Brakes squealed, and her body lurched again. The van moved forward and picked up speed. Minutes passed until it came to a complete stop. In the quiet, she heard an *Umph* and more labored breathing.

Moments later the back door opened. She felt herself yanked under her arms, carried like a stretcher, then dropped to the ground. A person on each side took an arm and dragged her forward. Soft dirt turned to grass then back to dirt.

A low screech of a heavy door sounded, and she felt the ground turn to concrete. Her feet scraped and banged on the unyielding surface. Missy tried to cry out, but the tape over her mouth blocked all but a groan. Air grew damp and musty around her. She could hear the echo of every step in the silence. Another door opened and light filtered through the stocking cap.

She squinted and struggled to focus as large hands yanked the hat from over her head, then stripped the tape from her mouth. Missy took a giant gulp of air and saw the crumbling walls of the warehouse. She felt the presence of someone who towered by her side. Ahead, two men stood under the flickering light of a lantern that rested against one wall.

She rubbed her face, feeling tracks of her tears and swollen eyes.

"Is this the one, boss?" The man grabbed Missy's shoulders and pushed her into an open area.

"She is, indeed," said another man, whose eyes were trained on hers as he approached from the shadows. "Good work."

It was the same gaze that had locked her into terror as she stood beside a closet door and a wide-brimmed rainhat in the Lucas house. No more pretend compassion or kindness, Jeremiah Lucas gloated over her, his prize. With Clarence at his side.

Questions without answers shouted over everything she saw around her. It was like the assault had robbed her of her brain. Was Clarence the one in the van? Or the one who'd grabbed her from behind?

"What are you doing here?" she asked Clarence. That was the real question. What was the kid she thought might be a friend, might have a real heart, doing here with his dad and her, a captive, at his side?

"That," said Mr. Lucas, "I can explain." But Missy didn't shift her eyes from Clarence. He stared at the floor, avoiding her gaze.

Another question rose up in grief and anger. "Were you there?" she asked, her voice rising into a shrill cry. "Were you at the river that night? Did you help him kill Ephraim?"

The room was silent. Clarence stood with his head down, clenching and unclenching his hands.

It would've helped if he'd thrown back some insults, protested, said she was crazy. But he didn't say a word and refused to look at her. Mr. Lucas held his hands behind his back, head held high.

"Do you know what he's been doing to those girls?" she yelled. "Tell me! Do you?" Missy hurled herself toward Clarence, her hands and feet still bound. He caught her and their eyes met.

"Enough." Mr. Lucas stepped in. "Time to stop this. Men, get her into the crate."

Hoisted up by the arms and legs, she braced for the impact as they tossed her body into wooden slats. She landed on one hip and cried out. "Help me, please. Don't let them do this, Clarence."

"You know what to do," said Mr. Lucas with a confident tone. No one was going to mess this up. He'd make sure of that. "Let me know when the transport is complete."

Clarence spoke in a low voice. She could barely hear him. Then his voice rose insistent, desperate. They were talking about her.

"Dad, she can't hurt anyone. This is wrong."

"Wrong? I see that you're worried about *the right thing*. An interesting turn of events. Since when?"

"She's my friend."

"Your friend, is she? Really. After everything I've done for you, Clarence. And now—to hear that your loyalties are divided. It hurts, son. It hurts."

Silence, then, "Dad…there has to be another way."

"Another way." Jeremiah Lucas laughed. "Hmmm. Yes, I believe there is. Men, help me out here. Clarence needs another trip down river."

Missy heard thrashing and crashing around the darkness. The wooden crate opened, and Clarence's body smashed into her side. A sharp crook of his elbow jabbed against her right shoulder. She cried out in pain.

The crate shook one more time and a thick leg pressed against her side. Finally, she heard the sharp staccato of a hammer nailing the crate shut.

Lucas shouted, "Leave them here. What happened to the barge? It was supposed to be here. Do I have to do everything?

"I'll handle this. You make sure the barge gets here and makes the pick-up. Then go find the other one."

Gwen. They were going after Gwen.

Footsteps faded and silence followed. She felt the heat of Clarence's body beside her and smelled acrid sweat. A deep heaving shook and filled the small space.

Jeremiah Lucas had thrown his own son into a wooden crate to be shipped down river. Just because he'd stood up for a friend. He'd used his son, then thrown him away like a Styrofoam cup.

Her heart ached. Not for the bully who'd tormented

her over and over, but for the boy who'd suffered so much. Missy remembered Pa planting a young tree on their property. He'd attached a metal rod with soft supports on each side of the tree, then hammered them deep into the ground.

"It's young and needs support," he'd said. "Otherwise the wind and rain twist the trunk and it won't grow straight."

What about Clarence? All those years of bullying were because a kid's heart had been twisted by someone who should've cared, who should've loved the one who was his own. Would Clarence ever be able to stand straight?

Missy was alone and helpless, just where Jeremiah Lucas wanted her. She'd tried to help Gwen. And gotten captured in the process. So much for helping.

The worst part was knowing what this would do to Pa. Knowing how he'd spend the rest of his life trying to understand what happened to her.

Clarence shifted and pushed her into one side of the crate. An awkward pressure against her backside broke through her thoughts. It was the pocket knife. If only she could reach it, they'd have a way out.

She peered over at Clarence in the dim slats of light. He was slumped into the corner with bowed shoulders and head down. Was he an enemy or only wounded and alone? She opened her mouth and the questions spilled out.

"How did he get you to help him? Did he hurt you? Is that why those bruises never really heal? Talk to me. Tell me."

Silence. Then a weary voice. "You don't understand. You can't."

"Can't understand? How you could be loyal to someone who hurts you, who makes you do bad things? What kind of love is that?"

Clarence spoke so softly, she wasn't sure she heard him. "The only kind I have left," he said.

"What about your mom? What about her?"

"She's gone."

"I know, but…" What could she say? He had no one. No one to fall into when he was shattered. No refuge, only the loneliness of the worst kind of betrayal.

She remembered how she'd felt after Pa was arrested and she'd had to go to the shelter. When she'd lost Ranger, and all the girls despised her. When even the people she thought were friends had left after they found out Pa was in jail. And Benjamin. Well, the jury was still out on him. Still, love had never left her. She hadn't been tossed aside like trash on the side of the road.

"Your mama loved you," she said.

"Maybe."

"How long has your daddy been doing this?"

"A while. Mother found out. She left me with him. Don't know why, but she did."

"Maybe she was scared and didn't know what to do."

"Whatever."

Words came out of her mouth before she could think, before she could figure out if they were right. Still, she knew they were true.

"It wasn't your fault," she said.

Silence, then a groan rose from deep in Clarence's belly.

"It wasn't. You couldn't have done anything else.

But now you can." Missy had wheedled the knife out and opened it. She sawed it against the ropes, trying not to cry out as it sliced her flesh and felt her blood mingle with the fraying fibers. She kicked once against the wall of the crate.

Nothing. No one responded from outside the crate. Even Clarence was quiet. She pounded harder against the wooden slates. They were thick and her legs throbbed, but she kept it up. Clarence shifted next to her and his leg extended beside hers. The whole crate shook as his legs pummeled it like a pair of battering rams.

Missy redoubled her efforts as he pulled back and slammed the wood over and over. A loud crack sounded in the night. They both paused, then kicked again. Dim light appeared from outside as the wooden slats gave way and they climbed out of the shattered crate.

Missy peeked into the night, looking for Mr. Lucas, for anyone who waited nearby. Nothing stirred around them in the deserted warehouse. She reached for Clarence's hand but grasped air as another figure approached.

"Where do you think you're going, son?" asked Jeremiah Lucas.

"Dad…"

Mr. Lucas pulled a revolver from his jacket and motioned to the broken crate. He nodded at Missy. "Get back inside."

"No, sir, I won't," she said.

"Clarence, put her in the crate. We don't have time for this," he said, sure that Clarence would do as he always did. Just exactly what he told him to do.

But he didn't. Mr. Lucas was angry and stepped

forward. "Stand back," he said to Clarence. "I'm not wasting any more time."

Missy grabbed Clarence's arm and pulled as she turned to run. Clarence stood firm with an iron grip. "Clarence, let's go. Now."

His eyes were two dark, empty holes. Then he hurled her into the darkness.

Missy heard a shot and cry as she escaped into the night alone.

Chapter 19

Black clouds churned in the night sky, and Missy heard a low rumble. Staying in the shadow of trees, she ran. She paused to catch her breath on the outskirts of town. A dog rushed at a fence, yapping and growling. No help there. Missy ran on, unsure when her adrenaline would fade, leaving her collapsed and in the open.

The wind picked up, and the temperature cooled with the coming rain. A raindrop plopped and trickled down her scalp. She tripped and twisted her ankle. Forcing herself up, she limped to the shelter of a large tree.

She needed to think, but breathing took all her effort to still her pounding heart. If only she could run home to Pa and Ranger. But they weren't there. Besides, Jeremiah Lucas would have someone waiting there, in case she showed up.

The gun had fired, and now Clarence was alone with the one who'd decided to sell him along with her to the highest bidder. She'd felt his body crash into hers in the same shipping crate. Jeremiah Lucas couldn't afford to let her live. He'd take down everyone around her to make sure she was silenced.

She could sit down and cry. But how would that help? She could run, but where would she go? Besides, her body was so weak she couldn't move away from the shelter of the tree. She huddled beneath its dense limbs, hoping somehow to gather strength but knowing she had nothing left.

Her back ached and her head hurt. She'd been grabbed from behind, bound up and dragged away to face Clarence and Jeremiah Lucas—then crushed to the core when she realized Clarence had been helping his dad. Probably all along.

Had Jeremiah Lucas shot his own son? If so, he'd be lying there bleeding. Clarence, betrayed by his dad, abandoned by his mom, now dying all alone.

Missy didn't know how, but she wasn't going to let that happen.

She'd go back and check on him. Somehow, she'd get him help, somehow stop the course of this rottenness that was too much for anyone to bear. She didn't know what had happened to Gwen. But Clarence was the one before her now, and she wasn't going to leave him alone.

What if she retraced her steps and was found by thugs sent by Mr. Lucas? She longed to stay under the shelter of the tree. Not go back to the place she'd been tied up and thrown into a wooden crate.

What would she do if Clarence was lying there dead? Or worse, dying and she had no way to help him? And wouldn't his dad be one step away?

She pulled herself up and walked behind trees, through alleys and every cover she could find until a flash of lightning highlighted the warehouse nestled in the trees below, then disappeared again in darkness.

She longed for her flashlight, any light. As if in answer, more lightning slashed the night sky, and her body shook with the crash of thunder that followed it.

Just as quickly, darkness descended again. She tripped on some unseen obstacle and fell to the ground.

It was hopeless. She didn't have her flashlight, had no way to find her way back to the warehouse. Darkness had cut her off and now all she could do was lie on her belly, cradling her head in her arms. Damp grass pressed against her cheek and her body wilted as if every cell in her body was emptied of life. She couldn't do it. Couldn't help him.

A flutter of wings rose nearby. What had disturbed a bird's sleep? The soft rattle of what sounded like pebbles rolled nearby. Then in the bobbing light of a flashlight ahead, she saw a dark figure rush toward her.

Adrenaline surged back into her body in time for a leap forward and then a sprint back into the darkness. She hurdled over river brush, skirted trees before their trunks smacked her in the face, and dodged in crazy circles before landing in a tangle of fallen limbs. Yanking her feet free, she grasped a clump of grass to stand back up.

A bullet whizzed by her left ear. She dropped to a crab walk, then drew in a deep breath, rose up, and kept running. Thorn bushes snagged her arms and face. The warmth of her blood trickled down one cheek and onto her neck.

Soft grass gave way to boggy sand as she ran until an exposed root tripped her and she hurtled forward, face to the ground. Her body refused to move, refused to obey. It was over.

The rain fell, spreading its hush around her. She curled against the trunk of a tree, its dark imprint looming above her. It reminded her of the tree outside her window at home, and the branches that had held her when her heart ached. It'd kept standing even after Mama was gone.

Missy stood and placed her arms around the tree in front of her, embracing its strength. The toes of her tennis shoes pressed into the scratchy bark and she scaled, scooting her arms and legs inch by inch until her hands met the knobby crook of a branch.

With one last burst of strength, she launched herself onto the limb. It held. One leafy branch, then another, she climbed higher and higher.

A crunch of leaves signaled his approach. She watched by the beam of his flashlight as he ducked his tall frame under the branches of a nearby willow. A low branch pulled on the rain-hat she'd seen on another stormy night.

She tucked herself closer against the massive trunk and stayed still.

"Missy? Where are you?" It was Mr. Lucas's voice.

You'll pay. You'll pay with the one you love most. The terror of that night came back in a rush. They were back at the river. And he was calling her.

Missy pulled herself closer into the foliage that hid her. Light flickered through the branches of the trees around her as he searched the darkness with his flashlight.

A strange calm settled over her. Maybe it was exhaustion. Maybe she was just too tired to let the terror take over any longer. It was only a matter of time and he'd find her. "We've been here before," she said. "The night you murdered Ephraim."

"I'm sorry it had to end this way," said Mr. Lucas.

"How else could it have ended?"

"You could've stayed out of all this. Ignored some things, so to speak."

"Ignore them? How could I when Pa was in jail? And when I thought it was my fault?"

"Well, yes. It helped when you cooperated with my plan and took the blame. Somewhat of a diversionary tactic. But you fell for it."

"I fell for it because I love my dad."

"Of course." Mr. Lucas shifted his stance, an instant of unease.

"I thought I knew you, Mr. Lucas. That you'd helped Ephraim with the shelter because you'd lost Lucy. Because you knew how it felt when you lost someone you loved."

"Love. Vengeance seems to come right along with it. Making someone pay for its loss."

"Making someone pay. You mean like me, when I saw you at the river. Why did I have to pay?"

"You were in the middle of something that needed vengeance. Or at least change."

"And that meant murdering a good man?"

"Good man. What is that, exactly? Ephraim had to go. He would've ruined everything with his moral self-righteousness."

"Moral self-righteousness? He was a kind, honest man."

"Whatever. You can't understand."

"Like Clarence doesn't understand. Probably Lucy didn't either."

"Clarence. He's been a good help to me in the business. Not especially smart, but cooperative. Lucy. She…anyway, that's over and done with."

The rain turned into downpour and found its way

through the branches, soaking Missy. She shivered and hugged her knees. His flashlight cast weird shape shifters through the leaves in the moonlight.

"Why don't you come out of that tree and talk to me face to face?"

Missy had to stall him. She'd stay in the tree as long as she could get answers. And stay clear of that gun. "You knew Ephraim's mama and daddy."

"I did."

"They raised you for a time?"

"Yes. Why?"

"I couldn't figure out how you and Ephraim knew each other. And how you turned out so different."

"Different? You mean because I'm a small-town lawyer and Ephraim's a hot-shot attorney from Jackson?"

"No. I mean because he was kind."

"Ah, yes. Kind, but foolish."

"Did you and Ephraim help raise money for that shelter to protect young girls?"

"We did."

"But he didn't know why, did he? Until later. When did he find out what that shelter was really for?"

"What do you mean, 'really for'?"

"Amelia, Danielle, the others…How did you get them away from their mamas? Did they come on their own or did you tie them up and cart them off, like me?"

"You, Missy, are a special case. The ladies I deal with aren't worth much. Except for the cash they bring in. It was lovely to know you, Missy. Very sorry that this will be the last time we chat." Mr. Lucas pointed the gun in the direction of her voice, but she'd already moved, up higher into the tree.

Lucas moved away from the tree to get a clearer shot, peering upward. He fell backward and the gun shot into the air, then landed to the ground yards away. She saw light from the flashlight jerk in a wild tango as he tried to regain his balance and pull his feet out of the mire, thrashing around and cursing.

Missy shifted forward outside the branches to see the flashlight acting like a spotlight on the unlikely scene below. Jeremiah Lucas yanked one foot, then the other as he sank deeper into the muck. It was quicksand.

His ankles, then calves disappeared.

Still cursing and struggling, he descended deeper into the sand. "Get me out of here!"

Weird flashbacks of Clarence's foot caught into a snare. His dad was snagged now. Would she be responsible if he died? Would she be a murderer, too?

Missy heard a low, guttural sob as Mr. Lucas continued to struggle. A crazy, senseless compassion rose up in her gut.

Then she remembered the feel of the duct tape on her wrists, her feet, her mouth. And the gun he'd fired in her direction. This man didn't deserve mercy. This was her chance. She could leave, and no one would ever fault her. She could turn and run to safety.

Instead, she shimmied down the tree and examined the ground. Was there more quicksand? She picked through, tipping one toe in front of her, then another. Mr. Lucas struggled only a few yards in front of her, his hips twisted and arms extended to grasp river grass, sand, and whatever he could to pull himself to solid ground.

"Quit struggling, Mr. Lucas. The sand isn't that

deep. You can get yourself out if you'll just lay flat."
She picked up a stick and held it out, leaning as close as
she dared to allow him to grasp it. He did, then yanked.

Missy screamed and plummeted forward, her body
falling into the quicksand.

Chapter 20

The quicksand's suction pulled against her limbs as she faced Mr. Lucas. The flashlight had fallen out of his grasp, but its light trained like a spotlight on them both.

She felt his hot breath and looked into his eyes. Dead, vacant hate stared back.

"Why did you pull me in? I wanted to help you."

"Help me?" Mr. Lucas laughed as if he was mocking a small child who'd fallen and couldn't get up. "Like you said, I can get out of this. You, on the other hand, will not. I thought you were different, Missy Needham. Different than the trash hiding out at that shelter. Home wasn't good enough, so they ran away."

She watched his sculpted features form an ugly mask. "I made sure she'd never leave me again. And I'd make her pay."

"Her?"

"Mama tried to leave me alone... with him."

"What did you do?"

"I stopped her." He put his hands around Missy's neck. The bony grip of his long fingers tightened into a vise. "I made sure Mama'd never leave again."

Missy struggled. She couldn't breathe or speak. He pulled her closer. She saw his perfect teeth, the clench of his jaw. She felt the force of his words hiss in her face.

"You've been such a disappointment, Missy. I

expected so much more."

Stupid. Idiot. Disappointment. The familiar shame rose up and etched itself on her face. It kept popping up, no matter how hard she tried to press it down. He released his hold, only a little, and laughed. Laughed at the pain she'd known for so long. The lie she'd believed had arrived in human form to strangle the life out of her.

Only this time she wouldn't let it.

The storm swirled around her, its cool air a release. She relaxed, and Lucas's grip loosened.

Lifting one knee, Missy jammed her shoe into his chest. With one last heave, she pushed herself out of his grasp. He grabbed her leg and twisted. She yelled in pain, then kicked him with the other foot.

His hands groped, found her pants leg, and pulled her toward him. She felt the flashlight near one hand, snatched it, and jabbed it in the direction of his face. He cried out and released his hold.

The wet sand fought against her every attempt to roll away. Rain continued to expand it around their struggle. It pressed around her legs, relentless, like a lake of soggy concrete. His arms searched for her, following her gasps for breath.

Missy closed her eyes. She remembered a Saturday morning in October and imagined its warmth against her skin. She and Pa had been out setting fence posts.

He'd said not to struggle. When quicksand threatened to take her down, to agree and lie down in its embrace.

She flipped over on her back and straightened her body out like plank. The sand released her feet. She rolled. Once, twice, again and again.

She kept rolling until she came to rest on a tufted bed of cattails. Pulling up on her hands and knees, she rocked back and forth, then collapsed. Too exhausted to struggle, she lay flat and looked up into the night sky.

Rain slowed to a drizzle. The moon came out from its thick cover of clouds and crickets began their song. A hoot owl called nearby. The river inched toward her and Lucas.

She didn't have any strength. Couldn't move one more time. Even the thought of Pa refused to resurrect her body's will to go on. "See you in a bit, Mama," she whispered.

Peace settled in and covered her like a shawl.

Mr. Lucas's voice cried out in the stillness. Like another time when she'd run for the green rooftop of home, pursued by the very one who lay nearby, caught in the sand.

Only this time, it was different. "Help me. Please," he said.

Orion, the constellation, appeared through the clouds. Mama'd said it was the Heavenly Shepherd. Always been there, only covered by the storm. Gray light dimmed its brightness as the heavens began their journey into morning.

"What's the whole story, Mr. Lucas?"

"It wasn't my fault. Ephraim found out about the girls. Threatened to expose me. I had no choice."

"How did you get him to the river?"

"Called him, said I wanted to talk things over. It wasn't hard to find help. He showed up, not expecting any resistance. I was ready. He wasn't."

The quicksand had been working its silent way, swallowing him to his hips. "Get me out of here, Missy.

I'll go to Sheriff Davis. Tell him everything."

A dog barked in the distance through the mist and the light that signaled morning. The yowling of a hound dog came closer and closer. She recognized that bark.

It was Ranger.

He bounded into the clearing and tackled Missy, licking her face, leaping up and down like a little kid out of school. Benjamin was behind him.

"Watch out," she said. "There's quicksand all around."

Benjamin picked through brush and scooped her up into a long hug. She rested on his shoulder, soaking in his embrace and shaking with relief.

Sheriff Davis emerged from the shadows with Pa at his side. Benjamin moved out of the way as Pa tugged Missy to himself and held her, mud and all, in one grateful jumble. She curled into his arms, never happier to feel them around her.

"I heard everything, Lucas," said Emmett Davis. "Got you on this fancy recording device. Have a few witnesses, too."

Mr. Lucas snapped, "Get me out of here! Immediately!"

"Not sure we can," Emmett said. "We'll try, though. You have the right to remain silent. Anything you say can and will be used against you in a court of law. You have a right to an attorney. If you cannot afford an attorney, one will be appointed for you."

Emmett studied the situation. "Before we get that rope to pull you out, you can tell us more about those girls."

"Get me out of here!"

"You murdered Ephraim," the sheriff said.

He knew. Sheriff Davis had heard him confess. She wasn't the only one who carried that awful knowledge. A weight left her chest and she breathed in the fresh air of a new day.

"He was going to expose us," Jeremiah Lucas shouted, like he was trying to convince someone, anyone. Missy watched him writhe against the quicksand, his voice raging against what held him captive.

"I'll give you names, just get me out of here."

It took a while to get rope untangled from the trunk of Emmett's squad car. Not much time to get names out of Mr. Lucas, though. By then he was swallowed up to his chest. Any deeper, Missy figured, and they'd just have to watch him go down, leaving only a rain hat as proof he'd been there.

Missy wouldn't leave Pa's side. He moved to make a loop in the rope Sheriff Davis extended. But each time he shifted his body, Missy leaned closer to him. She wasn't leaving him. Not now.

Emmett tossed the rope over Mr. Lucas's head. He managed to get the coil beneath his arms. It tightened, and Jeremiah Lucas groaned as the squad car inched forward, back end straining at the trailer hitch.

"Careful, boys," said Emmett. "Don't want to lose a squad car over this."

Missy wasn't sure Mr. Lucas's arms wouldn't pop out of their sockets. The car pulled forward, slow and steady. Mr. Lucas was released inch by inch out of the quicksand's grasp.

"Lie down, Lucas," said Emmett. "That quicksand won't ever let you go if you stay upright. Course, no skin off my nose if you choose to go under."

River's Call

Finally, with a giant thwack, Mr. Lucas's legs and feet popped out. The car kept pulling until his body lay limp on the damp ground. Emmett cuffed his hands behind his back. Then an officer on each side lifted him and half carried him to the backseat of the squad car.

Missy watched sand and mud drop in stinky dollops as they shoved Mr. Lucas inside. That was going to be one mess. Just like the one they were fixin' to haul away.

Emmett turned to Pa. "Meet me at the office? Maybe in an hour?"

"We'll be there."

"Pa, we've got to find Gwen. I think they took her. We have to—"

"She's safe with Sheriff Davis. Has lots of time to tell her story about Jeremiah Lucas." Pa's arm around her shoulders squeezed. "You can talk to Gwen tomorrow. It's been a long night."

He pulled her into another hug. "We gotta get you home. Have enough in you to talk to Emmett for a few minutes?"

Benjamin stood nearby. "I'll watch out for Ranger," he said. "You go on."

"Benjamin, I…" Missy had so much to say, so many questions. She didn't want to let him go without a thanks, at least.

He'd been a friend. In all the ways she hadn't. She'd cut him off without a word, without even letting him defend himself. All because she'd been scared. Sure that he'd found out the truth. That she was a disappointment waiting to happen.

But it was too much to say right now, to figure out how to put it in words.

He lingered for a minute, looking at Missy, then Ranger.

"Go on. I'll take care of her," said Pa. "Come by tomorrow. Your mom's worried."

Benjamin turned bright red and nodded to Missy. Missy wrapped her arms around Ranger's neck and nuzzled her face, getting a noseful of smelly, wet dog.

"Go with Benjamin," she said.

And he did.

Missy wondered how he and Ranger had found her. And why Benjamin had been out looking for her in the middle of the night. She and Pa headed to the pickup, where he pulled a jacket out and placed it around her shoulders.

"What happened to Clarence?"

"He's in ICU. Took a gunshot."

"It was his dad. His dad shot him." Missy's voice rose, panicked. "I've got to see him. He helped me. He pretended to hand me over to Mr. Lucas, then pushed me away and blocked the gunshot. I heard it, heard his cry…"

Her dad extended one long arm and drew her to his side in the truck. "Okay. Emmett can meet us at the hospital instead of the police station. I'll call him when we get home. Time for a shower and something to eat before we head over."

Sunrise began its break against darkness as Missy and Pa made their way back to the house. Eastern light shone a rosy glow over the white-framed house they'd called home. Home with Pa. Light had come with a new day and darkness couldn't do anything about it.

Not by her alone. But by a small army who'd gathered around her. One she hadn't even known about.

Pa flipped on the lights in the family room, turned a thermostat, and the old furnace hummed to life, warming the room and inviting them to stay. She looked upstairs, longing for her own bed.

But she had to see Clarence first. Missy rubbed her eyes and walked into the downstairs bathroom. Its cold toilet seat jolted her wet behind. Washing her hands and face in cool water, she looked into the mirror.

The freckles were still there. Her neck still stuck up like a swan's, extending to the crown of the same scarlet curls. She wondered how she could look the same. Hadn't something about last night's business left its mark?

Weariness crept in, but Missy shoved it back down. Straightening her shoulders, she lifted her chin and peered into the mirror. It was over. Almost.

Pa'd placed a small stack of clean clothes and pair of tennies by the bathroom door. She turned on the shower and stood, shaking, in the warm, cleansing stream. She stayed there until Pa knocked on the door. "Sheriff Davis is waiting."

They climbed back into the truck where Pa handed her a hot chocolate and small package of powdered sugar donuts. Her favorite.

Powdered sugar sprayed as she stuffed one tiny donut, then another into her already full mouth. "You're out of jail."

"Yep," Pa answered. He looked down at her for a moment and squeezed her shoulder, as if to prove to himself she was right there.

"Benjamin came looking for you at the shelter last night, Ranger in tow. He'd heisted his mom's car—something about an apology? Anyway, by the time he got to the shelter, he saw Adele hobbling around the front porch, looking like someone'd beaten her with a stick. Said she'd been drugged, probably to get to you. When they couldn't find you, she sent Ben to Sheriff Davis.

"Ben was driving to the station when he found Clarence collapsed under a streetlight. Saw that he was bleeding and took him to the hospital, then called Sheriff Davis. Said Clarence told him what happened and that his dad was on his way after you.

"That's where the ruckus began. Ben, bless his heart, had the presence of mind to get Clarence to the hospital and call the sheriff.

"But when it came to you, he roared into the jail like a house a'fire. Ordered Sheriff Davis around like a general on assignment. Ran down the hall toward my cell, Ranger yipping and howling beside him. 'We've got to go now,' he kept yelling.

"Well, you know how the sheriff moves like mud on a cold day. He let me out of the cell, said he'd explain later.

"No *later* with Benjamin. Said he and I were going on ahead. That Ranger'd find you. No matter where you were. And he wasn't waiting, by God.

"That's when I saw he'd been driving his mom's Lincoln. No license, no nothin.' Blood all over the back seat. Decided we'd better stay on foot and track the dog.

" 'Go find her, go find her, Ranger. Go find Missy,' he said. Had one of your hair thingamajigs— scrunchies? Guess you'd left it behind one day."

Pa looked at her with that wrinkle between his eyes. It'd been that day when she'd gotten mad and left—after the kissing. But she wasn't telling that part to Pa.

"Off we went, following your dog the best we could, while he yowled and hopped through the brush like a bunny on steroids.

"Sure enough, he found you. Sheriff Davis was right behind us, stayed hidden and recorded that last conversation.

"The long and short of it is this, Missy Needham." Pa looked over at her with something in his eyes she didn't recognize. "If you're looking for a friend—look toward Benjamin Eckstein."

Missy swallowed. She snuggled under his arm, moving her long legs away from the steering wheel. She was taller and was harder to fit than before he'd been in jail. Still felt like home, though.

"I'm proud of you, girl."

"Proud? But I messed up. I…"

"You faced down something way bigger than you. Took courage. Besides, I can be proud if I want to."

Before long, the pink stucco of the hospital appeared, and Pa pulled into the parking lot. Emmett met them at the door and, after a muffled conversation with hospital staff, motioned them toward ICU.

He and Pa stood face to face. This time was different. A new respect replaced the old hostility. Somehow the events of tonight had changed more than she'd imagined possible. "Thanks for taking care of my girl." Pa's voice shook, and Missy remembered that tremble in his lips when they faced each other at the door, Sheriff Davis with arrest warrant in hand.

Emmett Davis looked awkward, nodded, and shook Pa's outstretched hand.

A nurse arrived and motioned Missy to one of the rooms. It was quiet except for the beeping sounds of monitors. Missy felt her own heart beat in a rhythm mustered at the end of a long battle.

At one point she'd have been relieved to see Clarence laid out on a hospital bed. That was before she knew what life had been like for the bully, Clarence Lucas. How much pain he'd stuffed, with nowhere to go and no place to hide. Living with a predator who happened to be his dad.

She'd appointed herself judge and jury, too. Life had been easier to manage in black and white. In the last few months, good and bad had morphed into another category. Broken.

It was complicated, like Mr. Lucas had said. Most complicated for a fourteen-year-old son who'd lost his mama and had been cast off like an emptied Styrofoam cup by his dad. One who was shattered, but maybe not beyond repair. At least she hoped.

"We did it, Clarence," she whispered. "We did it."

Clarence's eyelashes fluttered as if a tiny breeze had settled over them.

Missy perked up at the movement. "You've got to make it. Not for me. You don't owe me. Well, maybe some for the insults and for that trip to the floor face-first.

"'Cept I understand now. You shamed me to prove I was the loser I already knew I was. I put up a fight 'cause on the inside I was so mad. Mad that you knew."

She wanted to shake him but didn't dare touch his still form. If only she could see movement, anything other than the unrelenting sound of monitors and the rhythmic rise and fall of his chest with the ventilator, tubes extending in every direction. She reached out to put her hand on his arm, then drew it back.

There was hurt all around and no way she could make it better.

"You can't leave. Not now."

A nurse stepped through the door. "Time to go, young lady."

Missy walked out of the room and plopped into a chair in the small waiting room. She stared ahead as Pa whispered, "Hey, squirt. You okay?"

She looked up to see Emmett walking toward them, puffy eyes and holding a cup of coffee.

His belly spilled over the sides of the orange plastic chair as he sat down like he'd been on his feet all night. He'd always looked too tired to smile, but a tiny grin crept around the edges of his mouth.

He started slow, rubbing his forehead and clearing his throat before he began to speak. "Missy don't know how long we've been working on this case. Had our suspicions, but no proof. I'd had to tell one too many mamas that their little girls were gone. I was done with it. Couldn't imagine my Allie in the hands of that pervert."

Pa nodded, cut his gaze to her before saying, "I hear that."

Emmett continued. "Lucas set up the shelter and used it to sell young girls to the highest bidder. Ephraim had no idea. Not until right before he was murdered. No one else did, either. No reason not to trust a man like Jeremiah Lucas. We were gettin' close, though, when Amelia disappeared." He shook his head, lips closed in a tight line.

"Turns out it was a massive ring," he said.

"Crossed state lines, covered a three-state area, and fixin' to get bigger. The network had so many tentacles it looked like an octopus. But we didn't know who was behind it all."

"What about the girls?" Missy asked.

"Some we'll be able to find," Emmett said. "Others...I don't know. We're getting that sorted out the best we can. Lucas gave us a lot of information, so that'll help."

"What about Lucy? Mr. Lucas said she'd—"

"Lucy was one of his victims. Turns out, so was Janie Truett. Lucy'd run from him one day. He snapped. We never found her body. Guess Janie had tried to leave one night at a party. Grabbed and pushed her into the river, let her drown. Saw nothing wrong—said they both deserved it for leaving him."

Missy could hardly process what he was saying.

"His conscience got seared until it didn't exist. He and his people targeted vulnerable girls and offered them a better life. They'd look for a weakness, find out what the girls wanted most. Then used the hope they offered like a trap. Or they'd use the shelter and kidnap girls they knew were already runaway risks."

"How long had it been going on?"

"Too long. The high school counselor, Mr. Wintroble, was involved. He helped spread a rumor about Ephraim. Although there were plenty of men who couldn't afford to be exposed along with Lucas. They came along with him that night at the river.

"We found files tucked away in a hidden drawer in Wintroble's home office. Implicates him with Gwen and several other girls. We'll be prosecuting him for each one."

Emmett shook his head and took a deep breath. "If it hadn't been for Missy, this thing would still be going on. And we'd still be in the dark."

"Were some of the men locals?" asked Missy.

"Jimmy Collins from the motel and Merle Owens from the drug store had a big interest in making sure Ephraim was silenced. The rest of the mob were low level criminals Lucas used behind the scenes to capture those girls. He was the one behind it all."

"I saw Mr. Collins at Ephraim's funeral," Missy said. "Mr. Owens, too."

"Probably keeping an eye on you."

"On me?"

"Lots of eyes were on you. More than either of you knew, that's for sure. Most everyone knew you'd been at the river, although they weren't sure what you'd seen."

"No small miracle she was kept safe," said Pa.

"Yes," Emmett said. "Jeremiah Lucas—for some reason, he... Well, seems that he targeted girls he thought were trash. Some kind of sick thing against runaways. Didn't feel that way about Missy. Not that he wouldn't have..." Sheriff Davis stopped talking when he saw Pa's face.

"I upped surveillance around your home and around Missy. When I found your knife at the river, I was bumfuzzled, for sure. Couldn't figure out why Missy would've had it. And how Ephraim's blood was on it. All the evidence stacked up against you, Hal.

"The more I investigated, the more I knew there was something I wasn't seeing. Didn't advertise that, though. Hoped an inquiry into an innocent man might help smoke out the guilty one."

Missy shot a glare toward the sheriff. "You figured out Pa was innocent?"

"I was pretty sure all along, but I couldn't ignore the evidence. I've known your dad for a long time. Sorry for the jail time, though."

Pa sighed. "Don't know whether to thank or slug you."

"That much hasn't changed." The sheriff's belly jiggled as he laughed. A lightness came into his face that Missy'd never seen. She'd judged him wrong, too. All those weeks without Pa had been terrible. But they'd been part of a real-life chess game that had finally taken down a vicious opponent.

Checkmate.

Pa's face shone with pure relief and joy as he laughed with the sheriff. "Funny how the same guy who pit us against each other in high school brought us together now."

"Something about that new place Mama talked about," said Missy.

"New place?"

"She told me an eagle uses a storm's wind to rise above it to a new place."

Pa nodded. "She was right." He rested his elbows on his worn jeans and turned her chin toward his gaze. "By the way, tell Mama you won't be seeing her for a while longer. She'll understand."

Missy covered her heart and looked up and around, like maybe Mama was nearby. Had Pa heard her thoughts while she'd beckoned to Missy overhead?

Maybe she'd been talking to Pa, too. Still alive by an invisible line that had kept them tied together as a family.

Emmett Davis pried himself out of the chair and stretched arms overhead with a giant yawn.

"Will you be needing her testimony?" Pa asked.

"Don't think so. The hole Lucas dug is swallowing him up right now.

"Funny how even dirt cooperated when Missy stepped in to do what couldn't be done. One thing I gotta say, though. It ain't pretty, but it's true. We gotta deal with it. Clarence worked with his daddy in the ring."

"What does that mean?" she asked.

"That means he'll be prosecuted, along with everyone else involved."

Chapter 21

Sunshine streamed through the windows of the ICU sitting room. Fatigue crept through Missy's limbs, and she struggled to sort out her thoughts. Not after all this. Not when Jeremiah Lucas had been caught and justice was beginning to shine.

"Even though he tried to save my life?" asked Missy. "And Pa's? He wasn't cooperating with his dad. I thought he was at first. But he pushed me away from the gun. He took the shot himself. That's gotta count for somethin'."

"Missy, Clarence helped his daddy."

"But he made him. I saw the bruises. That's why he missed so much school. Ask Miss Terrell. She'll tell you." She stood up and stomped her foot. "Nobody knows what he's been through. How he lost his mama and got stuck with a monster for a dad." She turned to her father. "Pa, can't we help him? He won't talk. We gotta be the ones who reach out."

"We'll do the best we can."

"The best we can ain't never been enough. And you know it."

"How many girls are safe at home now that Lucas is caught?" Pa asked. "We can't do it all. Neither can Clarence. He did his best. Love can be a muddy river— all our humanness and mistakes don't keep it from being love."

"I thought I could trust Mr. Lucas," she said.

Pa reached out and took her hand. "You and everybody else. Only Clarence and a few others in town knew what was going on. Somewhere things got twisted inside and shot out like a poison vine everywhere he went."

The drive home was a blur. Sadness had reached up and grabbed her gut. It climbed up her throat with a cry that had lost its voice. Pa held on tight, guiding her up the porch steps to the front door.

He helped her up the stairs to her room. Missy looked around in shock. A new pine dresser stood in the corner. A round table in the same pine stood by a headboard covered in soft lavender. Over the bed, a downy comforter with pinwheels of periwinkle and pink danced in tiny swirls of soft comfort. The palest blue sheets covered the bed and a new pillow. On the nightstand rested a brand-new whittling knife.

"Mrs. Eckstein's handiwork," Pa said. "You get in bed, but first, take this pill Doc sent over with a swallow of water."

Missy swallowed the pill, crawled under the comforter, and closed her eyes. In the next breath, she was asleep.

****

Missy slept through the next day and night. Now that Jeremiah Lucas was in jail, fear didn't run her body like a tyrant. A warm breeze drifted over her face through bright sunlight when she finally opened her eyes. Seemed like spring had arrived full force overnight.

Still groggy, she rose up in bed enough to peek out the window to the yard below. She didn't have to search around every tree or check out possible hiding places anymore, wondering if danger lurked.

Instead, Pa's azaleas bloomed like they'd been waiting for her attention. Their fuchsia petals filled the bushes and overtook tender green leaves, despite Adele's dire predictions of their potential demise.

When she finally stumbled down the stairs, Pa was already up, sitting at the kitchen table. Steam rose from fresh biscuits and gravy simmering on the stove. Sunlight shifted through leaves of the oak tree outside their kitchen window. A lacy valance matched panels over the side door. Looked downright fancy.

Pa read the paper, glancing up from time to time and looking pleased as she slathered gravy on a fresh biscuit and poured cold milk into her glass

They'd have lots of time to talk. Love had held the weight of all that mess. It stayed strong, even if it did get pretty muddy in the process.

After a second helping of biscuits and gravy, Pa gathered up the paper, put dishes in the sink, and grabbed his keys. He stopped and looked at Missy, as if unsure of what to say.

He'd taken off a few days from the mill. It was too soon for him to be headed off to work. She fought down a small panic that tried to rise up inside.

"Where are you going?" Missy asked.

"They're transporting Mr. Lucas this morning," he said with a tender look. "You don't have to go."

"I'm goin'. Give me a minute."

Bolting upstairs, she put on a pair of jeans and T-shirt, then rifled through the closet for her favorite tennies. Flashing back to that night, she remembered the shoes were still at the back door, a silent witness to the battle they'd shared.

She said a quiet thanks, then jogged downstairs with another pair in hand.

Pa stood by the truck as she ran out and slammed the screen door. Ranger took one look and leaped into the truck bed as they climbed inside. He licked the back window, tail beating and butt waving back and forth. Missy turned and held her hand against the window.

It was good to be home.

By the time they'd pulled into a parking place a block away from the jail, small groups of people had already gathered. They spilled over curbs and onto the cobblestone pavement of Main Street, chatting and looking toward the courthouse.

She and Pa excused their way to the sidewalk where Adele stood. She nodded hello and spoke in a low voice. "Hear they're expediting the trial."

"Know where he's headed?" asked Pa.

"Maximum-security prison in Boyertown," she said.

Missy looked up at Pa. Boyertown was in south Louisiana. They both needed to see him sent far, far away. Probably Adele did, too.

"What about Beatrice? Any word?" asked Missy.

"Only that she'll be tried as an adult," said Adele. "She was a big part of Lucas's network at the shelter. Got paid well for her efforts."

Adele drew in a long breath and Pa placed his hand on her shoulder. "It's over, Adele. None of us knew. But it's over now." Missy was surprised to see her extend one arm around Pa's back to receive his warm side hug.

Glass doors at the entrance of the jail opened, and a

small squad of officers walked toward an armored vehicle. A path had been cordoned off, but Missy wiggled her way to the front and watched as one of the officers stepped into the driver's seat and sat ready.

Other armed guards surrounded the vehicle, guns strapped to vests and visors covering their eyes through brown helmets. Two more state police appeared through the door with Jeremiah Lucas positioned in the center, his hands and feet in cuffs.

Cameras flashed. He wore a bulletproof vest over orange prison garb. All that security probably meant he'd become a target now that he didn't have any reason to hide the names of those who'd helped him.

Holding himself erect, he looked poised, as if he were ready for the beach. Only he didn't have his sunglasses to hide that arrogant stare. And nothing to hide the hate as he looked up and saw Missy.

A disappointment. What she'd always buried in her own anger, in her own fight against what she'd believed about herself.

She stared back and didn't flinch. An officer placed one hand on his head and another on his shoulder to place him inside the van, breaking their gaze.

Those words had come out of the mouth of a liar. Someone who'd used his own pain to make others suffer. His own hate had become the quicksand that finally stopped him.

Pa turned to leave. Missy tugged on his arm.

"I've got to see Clarence."

"Go on. Just come home as soon as you leave."

Missy walked the two blocks east until she saw the hospital ahead, then to the ICU where she pressed a buzzer by the door. A nurse saw her through a long panel of windows and motioned her through the double doors.

"Come in, Missy Needham." The nurse smiled and led her inside.

She followed the nurse to the semi-dark room where monitors beeped and tubes connected Clarence's still body to machines that breathed for him, gave him fluids, and kept every heartbeat monitored.

A woman sat by his bed, her features cut from fine porcelain. She wore a simple linen dress cut in perfect lines against her slender frame. Missy looked at her shoulder to see if that raveled seam was still there.

Clarence's mother stroked his arm. Something about her eyes looking down at her son reminded Missy of a time long ago when Mama'd held her. She'd gotten cocky on her bike, aimed for a downhill slope and couldn't stop. Well, she *had* stopped when she hit a tree. But not without a lot of blood.

It was a mama's cry wrapped up in a single gaze.

Jessica Daly Lucas looked up as Missy stood by the door. She seemed distracted, like maybe one too many nurses had interrupted her vigil.

"My name is Missy."

Clarence's mama looked down as if she was ashamed. Was she going back in her heart to a time she'd left her son with a predator?

Silent tears dripped down her cheeks.

"When I heard that you...that he'd been caught, I waited to be sure. Never trusted the law or anyone else to shut him down. When they had him locked away, I came."

Missy's words sounded like a megaphone in the quiet room. "Clarence will forgive you," she said.

The woman jerked like she'd been shot. She shook her head.

"It might take time. But he loves you."

Jessica Daly wept, tears streaking her flawless face. "I don't know how that's possible."

"Pa says love can be a muddy stream. Don't keep it from being love."

Missy sensed someone at the door. She looked up and saw Gwen, flames twitching on her forearms. She looked ready to bolt but stood tall with her shoulders back and head up.

"Can I talk to you?" she asked.

Missy was so relieved she almost ran over and hugged her. Almost. Gwen led her to a corner away from the nurse's station.

"What happened?" Missy asked. "Are you okay?"

"Yeah. It's complicated. You and I were in the middle of a lot. Couldn't tell you, though."

"Tell me what?" Missy saw a softness in Gwen's eyes.

"I came to the shelter as a mole for the sheriff's department a couple of days before you moved into my room," she said. "Sheriff Davis suspected a trafficking ring but wasn't sure if it was connected to Ephraim's murder. Adele was helping, too."

"Helping do what?"

"Protect you. And hoping to smoke out the kingpin behind the ring. Sheriff wanted me close to you, but not enough that anyone would think we were friends."

Missy thought for a minute. "You mean you don't really hate me?"

"Don't get the big head," she said, without a sneer or snort. "When Clarence showed up at the river with the three of us, I knew he'd heard enough to alert his dad. Wasn't sure if he would. Still, it was an opportunity to bring Lucas out into the open.

"If that happened, it was only a matter of time until Beatrice came after you. I didn't know how to get you out of that bedroom without telling you too much. Turns out that back porch was a great hiding place."

All this time, Gwen had been protecting her. Sheriff Davis, too. And Adele. How had they cared about her all along and she'd never noticed? What else had she been missing all this time?

She remembered the terror that gripped her belly when they'd taken Gwen. Must've been pretty close to love.

"I had a hiding place. But you didn't," said Missy, daring to touch Gwen's arm. "They came after you, instead."

Gwen flinched but didn't reach out to strike her down. "Beatrice slipped something in Adele's tea that night, so she was out like a light in her room. She didn't hear a thing."

"That's why she didn't answer me when I knocked on her door."

Gwen nodded. "Sheriff Davis knew what was going on, at least from the outside. He had officers stationed around the shelter and at the barge by the river. They got me out of that crate right after that creep nabbed you."

Missy's heart sank. Everything had been turned which-way. Her head threatened to go into spin mode, but she took a deep breath and looked around at her new reality. Gwen was a friend after all. And Clarence? He'd pushed her away from the gun. Maybe more of that muddy love.

All of a sudden, she was too tired to understand.

"Lucas got in touch with Beatrice right away at the shelter," said Gwen. "She'd been helping him from inside. I'd let it slip a few days before that you had a hiding place at the river. She probably told Lucas where to find you.

"The quicksand was an unknown. Well, among a few hundred other unknowns. Guess it cooperated."

"How did you find out Lucas was at the head of the ring?"

"You drew him out, Missy. That's the long and short of it. If you hadn't seen Ephraim's murder and hadn't figured out it was connected to the ring, we'd still be in the dark."

"Oh," said Missy in a small voice.

"I couldn't give away my cover. Had to keep my distance. Had to cooperate with Beatrice. It was my part I couldn't tell you about." Gwen crossed her arms and looked straight at Missy. "Look, don't know if this makes us friends. Don't expect it to. But thanks. You did good."

In typical Gwen fashion, she turned without another word and left.

A trellis filled with climbing roses rested against the front of the Eckstein house. It didn't reach to Benjamin's window, but it was close. She glanced back to the front door. This would not go over well with Mrs. Eckstein.

Benjamin had returned Ranger the day before without even coming in to say *hey*. He hadn't answered any of her calls. Now she was forced to clamber like a spider up a wall, praying the trellis held firm.

Angling the toe of one tennis shoe into a wooden slat, she grabbed two more with her hands above and kept pulling until her arms ached and thorns snagged her cheeks.

When she reached Benjamin's window, she looked inside and saw him sitting, book in hand and staring at the opposite wall.

"Open this gol'-darned window now. Hear me?" She shouted as loud as she could manage without hurling backwards into the garden below.

"What the heck?" Benjamin jumped out of the chair and reached over to push against the wooden sill. With one more heave, the window opened and the screen toppled, brushing one side of Missy to the ground below.

"Do you mind? I could use some help," she said, clinging to the trellis.

Benjamin extended his hands and pulled her over the windowsill. She crumpled on the soft carpet with the sheer curtains wrapped around her feet. With a yank of one foot, she heard a loud rip and watched as the curtain panel floated to the ground. The rod crashed after it. Like the end of a game of dominoes, the lamp from the end table hurtled to the floor beside her. Missy held her arms over her head, expecting the ceiling to cave in next.

Mrs. Eckstein ran into the room, hands on her hips and lips quivering. She looked like she was trying to suppress a laugh. Missy looked around. Was she smiling at her?

"Please use the front entrance next time, my dear," said Mrs. Eckstein. "Or I'll have to up my insurance policy. Benjamin, untangle your friend. I'll get a broom."

As she turned to leave the room, Benjamin unwound the fabric from Missy's feet with careful precision, a wrinkle between his eyes, focused on his work.

"Why have you been ignoring me?" she asked.

Benjamin frowned and sat back down into the armchair. The chair wasn't designed for two butts, but it'd have to do. She plopped down beside him and turned his face with one hand until his eyes met hers.

"I was supposed to protect you," he said.

"That's what all this is about? You were the hero. You showed up with Ranger. And if you hadn't been where you were, Clarence would've died. Besides, I was the dimwit who got mad. You were right—I was operating in idiot mode."

A tiny shadow of one dimple appeared on one cheek. "Look," he said. "I don't want you to change. I want you to…" He gulped as Missy held his gaze. You cared," he said. "That's why you made up that plan, even if you didn't know if it would work.

"So, that's what I did. Hotwired Mom's car and came after you. Figured if I brought Ranger, you'd talk to me."

Missy leaned over and kissed him. His eyebrows shot up, then he grinned and kissed her back. Mrs. Eckstein walked back into the room with broom and dustpan. Missy and Benjamin tried to pull away but were stuck against the overstuffed cushion and couldn't move.

"Dang," Missy mumbled. Mrs. Eckstein offered her hand and pulled Missy out of the chair.

"Umm, thanks." Embarrassment traveled like an

internal furnace in shades of scarlet from her neck up to the top of her head. Then she remembered the beauty she'd found in her room that awful night when she'd finally been able to crawl into bed.

"I love my new bedroom, ma'am."

Mrs. Eckstein nodded. "I'm so glad, dear" she said, still looking like she'd break out into a loud guffaw. "By the way, you're welcome in this house, Missy Needham. Just not here, in this chair, kissing my son.

"Benjamin, escort your friend downstairs. I have guests coming and need to get things restored."

Awkward.

Still, another new reality.

****

By the time she got home, Pa was scurrying around, filling a picnic basket with paper plates and plastic cups.

"About time," he said, tossing her a red-checked vinyl tablecloth.

She'd almost forgotten. It was the first party she and Pa ever hosted, smack-dab on the beach of her favorite cove at the river. They puttered around the kitchen, tossing in random picnic items, feeling at a loss about how to get ready.

Just as Missy wondered what they'd bring in the way of food—other than the green beans Pa'd been simmering all day, Adele appeared at the front door.

"I'm letting myself in," she said. She carried in a chocolate layer cake and homemade custard, looking like a kid on the first day of summer vacation.

Her denim shirt brought out deep turquoise in her eyes that Missy'd never noticed. Pa hugged her and kissed her on the forehead. "You're looking fine on this

Saturday, Adele."

"Thought you'd need my help getting ready for the party," she said, looking around the cluttered house and rolling up her sleeves. "I can see I came in the nick of time. Hal, take this vacuum cleaner and use it. And don't forget to get under that coffee table."

"But the picnic's outside." Missy started to grumble until she saw Pa salute Adele, then wink at Missy as the old vacuum cleaner roared into action. There was a new sheriff in town, and she was taking charge here, on their turf.

Felt pretty nice, actually.

Missy helped pull the coffee table over its worn place on the carpet. She tossed aged issues of the *Farm Journal* as he swished away dust with a wadded-up tea towel, then stacked new issues in careful precision around four plastic coasters. Adele scurried around the kitchen, making tea, getting ice into the coolers, and slicing fresh tomatoes.

Mrs. Eckstein and Benjamin appeared at the front door right after they'd high-fived each other and collapsed on the couch.

"Come on in, Madeline," said Pa.

Madeline? Missy didn't want to ask any questions that would scare Benjamin's mom away, though. Not when she carried a tray of fried chicken in one hand and a casserole dish of mashed potatoes in the other.

Getting everything toted down to the river was a noisy jumble of loading cars, driving to the pebbled beach, everyone talking at the same time. Kind of like family. The aroma of fried chicken, apple pie—Well, Missy ate like she'd never seen food before.

The best part of the meal, though, was the friends.

Friends who'd been forged in the fire and made it through to the other side. Pa was back home and she was, too. Didn't get any better than that.

"Somebody's here to see you," Pa whispered in her ear and looked toward the road.

Clarence walked toward her. A little unsteady, but still on his feet. His mom waved from the car.

"Come on—we've got plenty of food," Pa called to her.

"That's very kind of you. But we can't right now. Clarence wanted to stop by before we leave."

His denim jacket strained around one thick wrist. The other arm was still in a sling. Red, chapped hands stuck out, awkward, looking for a place to hide.

"I gotta' go to Boys Ranch down by Birmingham," he said, his eyes taking in the friendly crowd, some who waved, others who called out his name and beckoned him toward the picnic.

Missy couldn't think of what to say, but she nodded. Not that she knew he was leaving. Just wanted to give him time to talk.

"How long?" she asked.

"Don't know yet."

He was silent for a minute, then looked toward the car idling nearby. "Mom said she'd be here, though. Waiting."

Missy wanted to break into a happy jig, but she settled for a giant smile. "That's good. Real good."

Pulling up her shoulders, she looked into his eyes. She'd heard something about eyes being a window to a person's soul. If so, there was a whole world inside a kid named Clarence Lucas. One that was worth saving.

"I got something to say to you," she said, even

though she wasn't sure what. After an uneasy pause, she chose the one she'd needed to say for a long time. "Thanks."

"For?"

"For pushing me away from that bullet. For covering me that day at your house."

Clarence didn't say anything but glanced in her direction before looking away again.

"I understand," nodded Missy. "I do."

In a strange way, she did. Understood how a son would want to please his daddy. No matter what.

Clarence's face contorted. He turned to leave. She wanted to know about his dad. She wanted to say she was glad he wasn't going to a detention center, but a place where he'd be a part of a family. To learn what it was to love people, maybe even to trust.

"See you around," he said.

"Not if I see you first." Missy grinned.

As Mrs. Lucas pulled off the gravel road and headed north, a squad car approached from the other direction. The car slowed as it got closer. It was Sheriff Davis with someone in the back seat.

Amelia's thin face peered through the back window. Missy waved as she watched the car drive out of sight. The last girl who disappeared was the first to return.

Maybe she'd lead the way for more.

Chapter 22

As the sun went down, everyone lingered by a fire Pa'd built on the shore. She and Benjamin roasted marshmallows and slapped them between chocolate bars and graham crackers for everyone. When they finally sat down together, Ranger planted himself at their feet.

The sunset faded, the air crisp in the darkness. It was time to head home, but no one wanted to leave.

"See there?" Pa sat on one of Mama's quilts and looked up into the night sky.

"What?" asked Missy, craning her neck upward.

"Up there in the southwest. It's Orion."

"Orion means light of heaven," said Benjamin. "Babylonians called Orion the Heavenly Shepherd. Holding up an unbreakable bronze club, he's primed for a fight against Taurus, the bull."

Missy was silent. She'd seen that Heavenly Shepherd before as she lay on the wet earth, spent and ready to meet Mama.

"If you look in the middle, Orion's belt is a line of three of the brightest stars up there this time of year," he said, still educating them out of the encyclopedia stashed in his brilliant head.

Missy looked around the river with a happy sigh. All the people she cared about were here, right at her favorite river. Ephraim would have been there.

Probably was in one way or another. Like Mama.

Somehow, they were still together. And along with that Heavenly Shepherd, they were now at rest.

With their clubs nearby.

A word about the author...

A former high school English teacher, Laurel Thomas loves words and their power to convey story. She's written for inspirational magazines, ghosted nonfiction, and delved into her favorite playground—fiction.

When she's not with family or roaming the halls of Oklahoma State Bureau of Investigation as a chaplain, she's on her laptop doing what she loves most—crafting stories of ordinary people who face impossible odds to accomplish the extraordinary.